SURVIVORS' TALES

Compiled by Peter Long
Art by C.B. Linford

A twoonefive collective book

Cover design by: C.B Linford

Printed in the United Kingdom

Cover Art by
C.B. Linford

Stories, re-imaginings and poems compiled from the writers:

Amy Susana Cornock
Christopher Beames
C.B. Linford
C. S. Parks
Kimberley Deer
Laura Goodfellow
Leola Rigg
Mandy Kerr
Peter Long

and

Verity Kane

*For our partners, daughters, sons, fathers, mothers, friends
and tutors that have guided and supported us. Thank you
for the tea, coffee, whisky, requests for take aways and
chocolate and of course for listening to our ideas.*

Welcome to Survivor's Tales, the inaugural book by the Twoonefive Collective. We are a group of writers who first came together whilst studying Creative Writing with the Open University. While some of us have now finished our degrees and moved onto pastures new, we have remained friends divided by miles but united by our mutual love of writing.

Some might say that Survivors' Tales seems a strange title and whilst we may have not survived shipwrecks, famine, or earthquakes we have experienced the grief of losing loved ones, fought against life changing physical and mental illness, battled through lockdown and the self-doubt that gnaws away at every aspiring author to bring you this collection.

Within these pages you will find a diverse selection of genres and styles that will take you on a journey from Tuscany to Northern Ireland and Alabama, from the oceans to cities and deep into the woods. Some stories will challenge you; some will make you laugh, and some will make you cry.

Survivors' Tales is an invitation to revel in the power of imagination and the art of storytelling and we hope that you, dear reader, will enjoy our anthology as much as we enjoyed writing the stories and poems contained within it.

CONTENTS

AT THE SETTING OF THE TUSCAN SUN

by C. S. Parks

The elderly gentleman climbed the last few white marble steps to the veranda, feeling his age with the exertion. The heat of the midday Tuscan sun had cooled slightly, bringing the promise of a more comfortable breeze floating in on the evening air. He stopped for a moment to take in the view. The patchwork of rolling hills, neatly tilled fields and vineyards spread out before him, filling his view with every hue of green you could possibly imagine. The land looked young, fresh and fertile. He closed his eyes and breathed in the air. A delicate lavender scent filled his nostrils and imbued him with a wave of calm as he exhaled. He felt revived again after the thirty or so steps he had just climbed to reach the hillside restaurant from the streets below. He removed a handkerchief from the pocket of his olive-green linen suit, lightly dabbing at a few beads of sweat which had started to form on his brow. He then put the handkerchief to his top lip to remove the excess moisture that had formed just under his thin, silvery moustache, he was certain it gave him a passing resemblance to Clark Gable. Folding it neatly, he placed it into his top pocket again. His finger traced down a fine silver chain to a side pocket in his carmine waistcoat. He pulled out an ornate silver pocket watch. The savonnette was engraved with a ring of wheat surrounding a rosewood disk. In its centre was a single, purple periwinkle flower inlay. He pressed the latch, and the lid sprang open with a click. The clock face was just as detailed as the case. The bezel replicated the ring of wheat on the outside, and the hour marks were represented with fine, Etruscan numerals, etched on to a silver plate. In the middle of the face, the innards could be seen as the centre wheel, crown wheel and rachet wheel effortlessly ticked away the passage of time. He smiled to himself. He was a few minutes early. He liked to be punctual.

'Buonasera signore,' said the waitress, greeting him with a broad smile at the entrance. Her crisp, white shirt complimented her olive skin and dark, doe like eyes. Her hair was pulled back in a tight bun at the back.

'Buonsera signorina, ho una prentazione per il secondo a nome di Robin,' he replied almost fluently.

'Fantastico!' she exclaimed clapping her hands with glee. 'Your accent is coming along nicely Signore Robin'.

'Thank you, Lucia. But don't tell anyone I have been practicing all week,' he said as he winked at her.

'If you follow me, we have reserved the table with the best view for you.'

He thanked her and followed her to the table. The view was indeed breath taking. To the west, sat perfectly in the centre; surround by its world-famous vineyards, you could see the Basilica de Allucio di Campugliano. Its white dome standing proud in contrast to the undulating hills that encompassed it; casting a long shadow on the ground, as the sun traversed across the sky to complete its final descent. Robin noted that some of the milky white clouds had already started to gain a pink hue. Once again, he looked at his watch. It was seven thirty-three pm. Fashionably late, he thought to himself, although preferring to be early himself, he admired a certain aloofness that allowed a little lateness, reflecting that one should never show that one is too keen. He ordered a bottle of Carmignano for the table and waited.

Robin did not have to wait long. A few moments later, a lady in a red, shirred midi dress appeared at the entrance. Her salt and pepper hair flowed just below her shoulders, and a mallen streak off to the right-hand side gave her an air of dignity and poise. She laughed musically as she shared a joke with Lucia as she showed her to the table. Robin stood up and adjusted his waistcoat.
'Signore Robin. Allow me to introduce Signoria Helena,' she winked as she walked away from them.

They politely pecked each other on each cheek and sat down at their table. Robin noted her delicate floral smell, not perfume, he thought, possibly soap.
'I must apologise for being late. I got to the top of the stairs and I was, shall we say glowing. I thought that it wouldn't make a good first impression, so I took a minute to regain my composure,' she said.

Robin laughed. 'I felt the same. I lost count of the stairs halfway up. I hope you don't mind but I ordered a Carmignano for the table and if I may be bold, I have heard the lamb is exquisite.'

'Sounds perfect.'

A few minutes later Lucia returned with the wine and took their order. The veranda was starting to get a hum to it now. A large Italian family sat three tables away and the patriarch; a sturdy man with thinning, slicked back hair; laughed with joy as his little girl had put two forks into some bread rolls, making them looked like feet and she was making them dance. Further on still, a young couple sat opposite each other, hands entwined, engaged in an absentminded digital dance. It the far corner an elderly guitarist, with long white hair, tied back in a ponytail, started to gently caress the first notes of "Bella Ciao" on his Levin Guitar, filling the evening air with a mournful sweetness. Robin and Helena were deep in conversation, sharing memories of their favourite art works that could be seen at the Basilica.

'So why did you choose Tuscany? I mean apart from the obvious beauty of the area,' asked Robin.

'Well,' said Helena 'I think it probably started with my father. He was posted here during the war. He saw combat during the Battle of Garfagnana. He didn't like to talk about that too much. I know he lost some good friends.' Helena looked thoughtful and sad for a moment.

'Then he would talk about the 8th Indian Division's bloodless advance at the end of December. His company was assigned to them and as they passed through the towns and villages, he slowly fell in love with the area and the scenery. I remember as a little girl, he would say he wanted to go back and explore it more, see how they had rebuilt it after the war.'

'That must have a terrible experience for him. It is lovely that he could see the beauty behind all the horror,' said Robin.

'Indeed,' agreed Helena. 'So, when I was ten years old, we went on our first foreign family holiday. I was excited for my first flight and to see a whole new world. I wasn't disappointed.' Robin noticed her face light up at the memory.

'We stayed the first week in Florence. Now you must remember this was just as the Sixties were getting started. Italy had just thrown off the shackles of the war. To a ten-year-old girl it was like an explosion of colour and sounds. I remember nearly every café had Connie Francis' "Where the boys are" playing almost on a loop; my mother and father arm in arm singing along joyfully. It was such a happy time.'

Robin smiled 'That sounds wonderful, you said you stayed in

Florence for the first week? What did you do for the second?'

'The second week was more amazing that the first. We then travelled down to the coast. It was so beautiful. I still remember seeing my first sunset there. I didn't know that there were so many colours. I remember weeping with joy, wrapped in my father's arms.'

'There was a young boy a little older than me called Nicolo. We became firm friends that week, running around the village. He would have to work in his family's restaurant in the evening, but that wasn't too bad because it was the only restaurant nearby; my family ate there every night. He would sneak me chocolate ice cream when no one was looking. The proper Italian ice cream. Not the muck you get in supermarkets these days.'

'He sounds delightful,' chuckled Robin 'Did you stay in touch with him?'

'Absolutely, we would write to each other every month without fail. His letters were so beautifully written. Even at a young age he had a poet's heart, and he filled the pages with such sweet words.'

The door to the kitchen opened and Lucia carefully picked her way through the tables to theirs and carefully laid down two plates. The aroma of the lamb, with delicate undertones of garlic, lemon and rosemary, was a joy to the senses. It had a simple, rustic pleasure that came with a longing for the homecooked meals only a grandmother knew how to make. A side dish of Tuscan asparagus and roasted baby plum tomatoes completed the meal. The first couple of mouthfuls were eaten in complete silence, as Robin and Helena let the flavours pervade though their senses.

'So, did you ever see Nicolo again?' said Robin breaking the culinary induced silence.

Helena laughed 'Well, twelve years later I had just finished university and I decided to go travelling for a few months. I promised Nic, as he liked to be called nowadays, that I would stop by for a week. When I got there nothing had changed much at all, apart from everyone had grown their hair long. Nic had grown his out to his shoulders and was sporting quite a natty pencil thin moustache. I think we fell in love that week. He still worked at his family restaurant and they needed another waitress. One week turned in to two years; we married in the February of Seventy-five. It was a simple wedding at the beautiful, white-stone church about a mile outside the village. Life was just so perfect.'

Robin offered Helena some more wine and she readily agreed. The sunset had decided to be dramatic this evening, casting vibrant hues of smoky orange tinged with sultry reds. There was just a hint of the blue sky lingering on the horizon, feeling a little inadequate, it desperately tried to hide behind a passing cloud. Robin placed the bottle on the table carefully.

'Do you mind if I ask? You said two years? I presume that you didn't stay in Tuscany?'

'Sadly not,' Helena replied. Her eyes lowered and looked to the side. The merest hint of a tear hung in the corner of her eye. 'Not long after the wedding, my father became desperately ill. My mother couldn't cope on her own, so we needed to moved back to England to help look after him. He lasted six long years before he passed away. By then we had started to build a life there. We had twins that had just started school. I know Nic often missed his Tuscan life, but he never complained or moaned once. We would go back once a year for a holiday, strangely it always felt like coming home.'

'I can imagine. That must have been wonderful for your twins. What are their names?'

'Erica and Jon,' Helena replied, the corners of her mouth turned upwards, and her eyes sparkled at the thought of them. 'One of each, they loved their Tuscan adventures. Especially Erica. She was her father's daughter. They would go off wandering the countryside for hours on end. Jon was like me. He liked to sit in the sun and read a book. Life was good.'

Helena paused for a moment, lost in a deep reflection. Robin noticed words, seeming ready for articulation, drop away hurriedly from her lips. Her eyes glazed, staring off towards the setting sun, the flame red sky reflected in her iris, finally she spoke.
'Remember I said Nic had a poet's heart?'
Robin smiled softly 'I do.'

'Poet's hearts are fragile, delicate hearts. Nic's was no different. I lost him two months after his sixtieth birthday. He was playing tennis with a friend and his heart broke. My heart broke that day as well.' Helena wiped a tear from her eye before it had a chance to escape to her cheek.

'I am so sorry,' Robin said, 'He sounded like he was an amazing husband and father.'

'He was. My biggest regret was that we never got to return to Tuscany to live. I know he didn't have any regrets but still it filled me with sadness. After his cremation we took his ashes and spread them by a cypress tree at the back of the church where we got married. I read out one of his short poems, a haiku, as the sun set. Would you like to hear it?'

Robin smiled and nodded.

'As Tuscan heart beats, At the setting of the sun, I fade to sweet sleep.'

'That is a beautiful poem,' said Robin. 'He was very talented.'

Helena smiled 'He was.'

A flock of birds flew high in the sky, making their final preparations before their night-time roosting. The sun's last chord was just peeking over the horizon, which was now a dusky, greying salmon colour. The guitarist started to play "Con te partiro" softly and sweetly. The veranda had now quietened to a low hum as everyone stopped respectfully to listen.

'So, you asked why Tuscany. I found love in Tuscany. My heart has always been here, I feel close to Nicolo when I am here. When I got my diagnosis…,' her words trailed off.

Helena regarded Robin for the first time properly. They had only spoken about her life; her strongest memories had been laid bare over the course of the evening. Her life had flashed before her eyes. She finally understood.

'Is it time?' she asked.

Robin smiled kindly 'If you are ready? We have another moment before the sun sets.'

Helena looked towards the setting sun. Its final glint of light resting on the landscape like a candle flickering before it has burnt the last of its tallow.

'I am ready.'

Robin smiled and opened his pocket watch. He reached out his hand and held Helena's in his. As the second hand reached the crest of the hour, a gentle breeze flowed across the veranda. Helena took a deep breath. Her body became dust on the wind, flowing over the dark Tuscan landscape.

Robin wiped a tear from his eyes, as she faded from view. He stood and adjusted his waistcoat and replacing the pocket watch in the side pocket walked towards the exit.

'Arrivederci Signore Robin, I hope to see you again soon,' said Lucia as he passed her.

'Not for many years yet, my dear, not for many years,' he replied with a smile.

BENEATH

by Mandy Kerr

The water's surface, grey, still, glassy. Mirroring the dark blue skies above. Beneath, the memories of a thousand frenzied fish, rolling and frothing, in the days before pollution closed the floodgates and the factory finally shut its doors. In the oiliest depths, one remained. Its genes flawed, its helix twisted and warped, feeding off the toxic chemicals, and the guts, spines, and fins of its long dead brothers.

 The longest, hottest summer for many years had seen the nearby community of Harrison, Alabama, already suffering the afterburn of job losses, wither into a virtual ghost town. Ramshackle buildings, sun-bleached and neglected, studded the main street like rotten teeth. Only one business remained open, a general store, Mason's, its awning faded and flapping in the scouring wind. A dog-eared poster, curled in the corner of a window, heralded the long-forgotten arrival of the Moscow State Circus. The grinning ringmaster winked into the sun; his scarlet coat blanched to pink. Old men, too old or not wise enough to move on or to find jobs elsewhere, gathered on the dusty forecourt in the late afternoon shade. Muscle memory and beer drew them here to sit, smoke and reminisce until dusk rendered them insubstantial as ghosts and they drifted unsteadily back to their homes.

Martha Mason half-heartedly wiped a cloth across the scarred countertop. The glare of the sun, diluted through the grubby windowpanes, became watery light which rippled around the shop, casting shimmering shadows across the shelves. Unmarried and childless, she was the last of the Masons and the store would die with her, its death rattle also no doubt spelling the end of the town of Harrison. Her brow creased as she thought of the woman who had just stumbled from the store. Poor Kelly. Abandoned by her good for nothing husband while in the family way, and now trying to dissolve her pain in cheap liquor. Jim had been neither use nor ornament, and it had been a blessing of sorts the day he had vanished, but his wife had struggled ever since. Martha knew how she paid her way, options were as scarce as hens' teeth these days, but never one to judge, felt only pity for the girl and her young son. Maybe tomorrow she would take the kid some sweets, Lord knows he deserved a little treat now and then. She patted some loose strands of hair back into her loosely coiled bun, brushed down her apron and with a sigh, turned on the old Bakelite radio perched on a carton of cigarettes. The plaintive voice of Patsy Cline drifted across the empty aisles, accompanied by the lazy whisper of the ceiling fan overhead.

The pool, on the outskirts of the once thriving community, had become an incubator, nurturing the creature in its poisoned womb. As it grew, so did its hunger, and the scabby pond floor became littered with the indigestible remains of whichever poor animal had unwittingly strayed too close to the water's edge. A dog collar, the antlers of a brave young buck, even a prosthetic limb lay semi submerged in silt and sludge. The creature had no name, no species, no genus. It felt, saw, and thought nothing. It merely fed and grew.

 In an almost deserted trailer park, midway between the town centre and the old fish farm, Joe carefully coloured in the last picture in his book. He painstakingly kept inside the lines, tongue slightly protruding, his grubby fingers gripping the blue crayon tightly. They had been a gift from his dad on his last birthday, presented with a grin and a ruffle of hair, and now worn down to waxy stubs. The drawing was of an underwater scene, populated by happy dolphins and mischievous whales. An octopus was playing the drums while a mermaid sang her siren song to an audience of multi-hued fish. Joe was old enough to question the reality of this scenario but young enough to hope that it was possible, and that somewhere out there, beyond the confines of the dusty trailer park, talking animals and friendly sea creatures really existed. His mom would tell him to grow up and not to be so stupid, but Joe hung on to his hope regardless. It seemed that his mom didn't believe in much of anything anymore. Joe closed his book and arranged his crayons back in their box, reds at one end, purples at the other, like a rainbow. His mom would be cross if he didn't tidy them away and he was trying very hard to not make her cross. Within the pressure cooker of their small caravan, his mother's temper had been steadily boiling to a fever pitch over the last few days, and she had returned earlier, slurring a few snarled words to Joe before shutting herself in her bedroom.

Restlessly, Joe searched the cramped trailer for something to do. Martha had recently brought him a jigsaw from the store, a smiling cowboy sitting proudly on a horse, as brown and shiny as the toffee his mom used to make, but he'd completed it several times already. Besides, there was a piece of the cowboy's face missing, so it never felt properly finished. His nose wrinkled at the acrid stench of empty beer cans and crusted fast food cartons piled up in the refuse bin. An ashtray crowded with scarlet tipped cigarette ends sat on the countertop, and a lazy fly wandered across its sticky surface. Joe's stomach turned over at the combination of the relentless heat and odours. A muffled thump came from his mum's room.

'Joe! Joe, are you there? Where are you?' Joe flinched at her voice, shrill through the door. He stood frozen to the spot, unsure whether to move, whether to reply, what to do or say. Several different outcomes played through his head, none of which ended well for him.

'Joe! Answer me, where the hell are you?' Joe tried to swallow, but his mouth felt like sandpaper.

'I'm here Mom.' His voice emerged as a strained whisper through his constricted throat.

'I'm here!' This time stronger.

'Well get the fuck in here. Now!' Joe looked at his mother's door at the far end of the trailer. It felt as if he was seeing it through a fisheye lens down an endless corridor. Before she had the chance to shout again, or worse still, appear in the doorway, Joe spun round, slammed open the caravan door and threw himself out of the trailer's stifling heat into the park, sending clouds of orange dust pluming into the air as his feet hit the ground and he began to run.

The air around the pool hung thickly hot, and even the vegetation and reeds skirting its edge lay limp and defeated on the pale banks, as if the effort of pushing through the atmosphere was too much. The silence roared. No sound of insects chirping or buzzing. No snuffling shrews or scrabbling rats. No birdsong. Where once men laughed and shouted while they scattered feed, and the water's surface was alive with the frenzy of a thousand quicksilvered fish, now just silence, as if the world was holding its breath.

Joe ran until a stitch beneath his ribs dragged him to a halt. He threw himself down onto the scrubby grass and lay flat on his back gazing up into the sapphire sky. Small clouds scudded across the blue, swept by the same arid wind which swirled the dust into eddies of red and prevented crops from surviving. Without the fish farm as a source of employment and stability, the town was nothing more than a desert, its future as bleak as its landscape. The sun's brightness cast prisms through Joe's eyelashes, causing him to see as if through a rainbow. He searched for animals in the clouds and found them. A cat with a curling tail, a unicorn galloping after a polar bear. A multi coloured shoal of fish, chasing and darting through the sky's ocean.

Joe got up and brushed the dust from his shorts. His mom would be even angrier if he came home covered in dirt. His trainers were already filthy, and the soles were coming away, so that small kernels of grit had worked their way inside and he felt like he was walking on broken shells. He carried on down the hill, scavenging his way through the bone-dry weeds and grasses surrounding the derelict buildings and ponds of the farm. He picked up and examined stones and bottle tops as he went, discarding some, but collecting the best ones in his pockets, imagining that they were coins and jewels and that he would be rich. He could buy himself a horse, or even a unicorn, and ride far away. Far away where it was quiet and cool, and he could eat sweets whenever he wanted. Where nobody shouted at him and he could leave his crayons out.

In the depths of the pool, the creature was nearing the final stage of its metamorphosis. Pectoral fins had become elongated appendages, strong and jointed, flexing against the pond floor. Claws scrabbled, becoming sharp against the rocky surface. Amphibious lungs flexed. Soon the pond would no longer be a prison.

Kelly clutched at the doorframe of the bedroom, swaying gently. The walls of the trailer seemed to lean in towards her, conspiratorially whispering their secrets. She shook her head and tried to clear her vision, to focus. Aspirin. She needed aspirin. She popped a couple from their blister and grabbed a half empty bottle of Coors from the work surface. Or was it half full? She chuckled to herself. Definitely half empty. The beer was warm and flat and smelled unpleasantly of yeast, but she washed the pills down with a couple of large gulps. The heat of the trailer coiled round her and squeezed. Taking a fresh bottle from the fridge, Kelly pressed it against her forehead. The condensation trickled down her face leaving cool, refreshing trails on her skin. She caught a glimpse of herself in the sunburst mirror hanging above the tarnished sink. Her hair, as flat as the beer, stuck to her face in stringy ropes. Her hand fluttered to her head to smooth back the bleached blonde strands, and she winced as she noticed the chipped varnish on her ragged fingernails. Bob would be coming over later, so she needed to smarten herself up. And fast. Kelly stared into the dark eyes of her reflection and wondered who she had become. The woman in the mirror stared back.

The boy. Where was the boy? She glanced around the lounge, annoyance starting to simmer up within her. His box of crayons sat neatly on a closed colouring book, carefully placed so the corners lined up. Her lip curled. The very sight of them reminded her of Jim. The trailer door was open, slowly swinging back and forth in the wind and Kelly stood in the doorway, scanning the scrubland, a frown etched on her brow.

'He'd better not be down at that damn pond', she muttered under her breath, thinking about the old boys and their store front gossip. They came out with some real humdingers, nothing better to do with their time than jaw like old women. Still, she shouldn't complain, they kept her in beer and paid her bills if she was nice to them. Sure, since the fish farm had shut down, several townsfolk had vanished with not so much as a word, but Kelly had always put that down to midnight flits by desperate men or those taking the opportunity to start afresh. To ditch their responsibilities like Joe's bastard of a father had done. She had thought Jim had been happy enough, that they'd both been happy enough. The grass was always greener for some men and Kelly supposed that when you lived in a desert, any grass was better than none at all. She needed another drink. Taking a last quick look around, she shrugged and turned to go back inside. He'd come back when he was hungry enough, he always did.

Joe liked it here, down by the pond. It wasn't cool but it was quiet. So quiet. Around the pool's perimeter, a chain link fence and hastily erected warning sign had long since collapsed to the ground in exhaustion, making it easy for Joe to explore his kingdom. With his newly acquired fortune heavy in his pockets, Joe felt like a king, like the last living being on the earth. He wandered closer to the pond. A languid, liquid sound caught his attention, and he approached the water. He knew that there were no longer fish there, that they had all died after some kind of accidental poisoning. His mom had told him that the poison had seeped into the ground and that the farm had closed rather than cover the cost to have it all cleaned up again. Joe had thought that was a shame. She'd also told him never to play near the pond, but he wasn't that near, was he? He heard the sound again. A wet slap, as if something had briefly broken the surface. The image from his colouring book filled his head. The cheerful underwater concert, dancing dolphins and the drumming octopus. For a second, he forgot all about his pockets full of riches, forgot all about escaping far away on a rainbow horned unicorn. Maybe the world of talking animals and friendly creatures existed after all. Maybe they'd been on his doorstep all along. Maybe his mom was wrong.

Edging closer, Joe stared in wonder at the surface of the water, grey, still, glassy. Mirroring the dark blue skies above. Beneath the surface, beneath the memories of a thousand fish, the creature in its birthing pool prepared to take its first breath.

THE WOLF INSIDE ME

by Verity Kane

Crazy glazing is in my lung,
broken glass pattern on the scan.
Crackling noise from where I once sung,
shuffling on when before I ran.

Broken glass pattern on the scan
mottled legs and a butterfly face,
shuffling on when before I ran.
The wolf inside me gaining pace.

Mottled legs and a butterfly face
aching joints and a throbbing head
the wolf inside me gaining pace,
still waking up, I'm here, not dead.

Aching joints and a throbbing head,
blurry vision and short of air,
still waking up, I'm here, not dead;
I look well but life is unfair.

Blurry vision and short of air
my heart is beating way too fast,
I look well but life is unfair;
my future looking overcast.

My heart is beating way too fast,
crackling noise from where I once sung.
My future looking overcast
this crazy glazing in my lung.

HALLOWEEN EYES

by C. B. Linford

They say that monsters only emerge in the dark.

That, no matter the circumstance, the light of the sun will chase the demons away; the beings with their gnashing teeth and their glowing eyes and their sharp, sharp claws, able to rend flesh from bone and blood from vein.

They lied.

Monsters are everywhere. What they don't tell you is that sometimes they're created deep inside, swirling blackness coagulating and filling you up until you feel them in every pore; until you're drowning in death and disruption and can no longer look in a mirror because the person staring back at you just isn't yourself-
I throw yet another veil over yet another mirror, and stare in silence as the reflective surface is shut away from the outside world.
I know monsters, I think, as I lace up my boots and throw on my cloak.

I know monsters. I do, I do- black eyes and thick fur, too many legs, gurgling snarls and destruction in their hairy hearts.
The door to the cabin groans mournfully as it swings open. I sling my rifle over my broad shoulders. A click of the tongue and my

hound, Gunner, is at my side panting and raring to go.

I hunt monsters.

He's been running from us for months now. A chase of rabbit and wolf with an inevitable end; the barrel of a gun pointed between hollow eyes. That's how it always ends. I find them. I shoot them. They die.
I forgot I was meant to grieve for them a long, long time ago.
'They might be monsters, Kahari, but they still breathe, like you and me. They still feel; the wind still blows across their skin. They see the same sun.'

'Then why do we hunt them, pa? If they're like us?'

'Some monsters can't be saved.'

'Some? So not all?'

'We look after our own, Kahari. We do what we must. We can grieve for them, even love them; pity them- but it's in their nature to kill.'

'We kill too, pa- we kill too.'
'To survive.'

To survive, survive, survive- to live and to breathe. As though they didn't take, take, take.

A full day of tracking brings us to a wide clearing by nightfall; it's quiet. Pine needles litter the ground, creating a soft bedding. The trees loom around us like silent guardians.
I crouch down by the fire I've set to cook the rabbit I caught. Half goes to the dog. I stare down blankly at my own, into burned flesh, and wonder what the rabbit felt as the bullet thudded into its head.

When sleep eventually comes, it's fitful; filled with wolves and white teeth and glowing orange eyes.

* * *

The low snarling of the dog is what wakes me. Sharp; alert. Heart thumping against my chest like a caged beast. Grabbing the rifle by my side I stumble to my feet, cocking it to my shoulder and turning in a slow circle to stare into the rippling darkness beyond the looming trees.

'Heel, Gunner.'

He presses his warm side up against my leg. His ears are flat to his skull; hackles up, tail bristling. He's never wrong.
Movement; Behind- I turn. Gun up. Something strange and shifting darting between the trees, hard to follow with the naked eye. Barely making a sound as it moves. I've never seen anything like it.
Gunner starts to bark and the creature surges into view stepping out of the treeline and into my sights and-

I freeze.

Humanoid, it's... faceless. Black body dripping excess like thick tar. Its limbs are too long, and it floats about a foot off the ground. Sightless, it still seems to stare directly into my soul. My hands are trembling so bad I nearly drop the gun. A numbness creeps up through my arms and into my legs and I find I can't move.

The creature approaches me. It moves in jolting, shuddering motions, dropping down to drag itself across the ground with elongated arms. A strange wailing sound escapes its throat. I take a stumbling step back. I fall. My lungs feel like they're filling up with ice, making it harder and harder to breathe as it grows closer and closer to me, Gunner continuing to bark and whine as he presses his warm side up against me, trying to shield me from the monster.

'Death follows,' a grating voice, gravelly and dripping with venom. 'So many lives taken. All you. All you. You are the snuff to a candle, the axe to a tree, the river to the bank. Eroding and soulless and cold. You take, take, take...'

'No, I- 'my voice emerges hoarse, months of disuse, desperate and fragile. 'I've done nothing, I- nothing- '

'You are the flame to kindling, the light to shadow, the cloud to the sun. Nothing lives. You are completely alone.'

'I'm not- 'but I was. I was alone. I'd been alone for years, since my father had died and passed the mantle to me. I only had Gunner.
'Ah... lies. Lies and more lies. But you know the truth, don't you?' It reaches out with an emaciated, tar slick arm, spindly clawed fingers brushing my cheek. I shudder and retch; they're cold, and the stench of decay and rot floods my sinuses. 'Come with me. I'll end it all. Your suffering, your pain. No more numbness, no more death. Only peace.'
I feel myself caving to the voice. Somehow sweeter. Somehow a caress to my weary heart.
It's closer now. Empty face inches away; cold seeping into my bones...
A rustling to my left. The creature and I turn our heads sharply in sync.
Halloween eyes. White teeth. Thick black fur. Bigger than a horse. Saliva dripping from an open maw. I find strength enough to clutch my rifle as the giant wolf emerges from the treeline, a deep growl shuddering from its chest like an engine.
The creature releases a high-pitched screaming wail, darting away from my body to face the wolf. Heart and teeth bared; he attacks.
The wolf leaps across the distance within seconds, body slamming

into the hovering creature. I see fur fly, blood splatter greying grass, screams and howls and grunts filling the sharp air, crunching and squelching and then-

It's over.

The creature flies, sobbing, back into the woods. The wolf, holding up an injured paw, turns to stare down the shaft of my rifle, pointed clean between his eyes.
My breathing is fast and uneven as I gaze down the sights.

We lock eyes.

Gunner growls.

I don't shoot.

I don't shoot. Survive, survive- I don't shoot. Shoot the wolf. Shoot the damn wolf!
He turns, tail low, and limps slowly back into the treeline. I watch him go in complete silence.

Shoot him. Shoot!

Only the breeze whispers through the trees as they sigh with relief.

I drop the rifle.

I sob.

Survive, survive, survive.

❋ ❋ ❋

Sleep doesn't come easy. My dreams are filled with wolves, circling their warm bodies around my own, hurling their soulful songs to the full bright moon above. Somehow, I find myself singing with them and among their songs I feel forgiveness, as though they are saying; It's alright, it's okay; we all make mistakes. You are safe here. We have you, we have you, we have you. We love you. One of us; pack, pack, pack.

I wake with a start. Gunner is growling low in his throat, laying protectively across my legs. For a terrifying moment, I think the creature from the night before has returned. Instead, when I sit up to try and find my gun, I lock eyes with a man.

A very shirtless man- covered in scars layered over dark skin; deep, warm brown eyes studying me with what I can only recognise as curiosity.

My gun is in his lap.

'You're naked,' is the first thing I say. It's not what I meant to say. I'd meant to demand he give the gun back- tell me why he's here.

'I am.' A deep, husky voice, with the remnants of a growl in his throat.

'It's cold out.' I respond, tongue betraying me a second time. My heart is fluttering like a caged bird. I'm in danger. It's then that I notice his hand; he's holding it close to his chest, and it's covered in blood.

'It is.' The barest hint of a smile on full lips.

I try to relax and take a moment to examine him. His hair is shaved at the sides, but full, wild, and curly on top. Those eyes, long lashed, haven't left me once. He's well built; muscle and a light layer of practical fat. Tall, I think, if he stood up.

'You're hurt.' I state.

He looks down at his hand. 'Banshee got me.'
'Banshee?'
'The creature. Last night.'
'How did... How do you know what... that is?'

'Because I manifested one myself a few years ago. Vile things. Crawl right out of your deepest fears and darkest thoughts.' He looks back to me, and I feel the tension return to my shoulders.

It takes a long moment for me to realise what he's saying. 'I made that.' Voice softer than the pine needles we're sitting on.

'You did.' He grimly confirms. 'They're created from our deepest, darkest fears and regrets. They hunt you down until either you're dead, or it is.'

'So it'll be back?'

'Probably.'

'How do I fight it?'

He tosses the rifle and I catch it mid-air.

'Put a bullet in its head.'

I gaze down at the rifle, running my fingers along its cold shaft, then turn down my brows and sharply look at him. 'Why would you re-arm the person who's been hunting you? For months?'
He tilts his head, and for a vivid moment I can see the wolf in him; I'm almost endeared, until I force myself to remember he's a monster.

'Because' he says, standing up. 'If you were going to shoot me, you

would have done it while you had the chance.'
'I have the chance now,' I say, hands gripping the rifle a little tighter.

'You do.' He agrees.

We lock eyes again and stare for what feels like days.

'Why did you help me?'

He shrugs. Turns away. I try to stop my eyes from trailing lower, over firm back muscles and strong thighs. He is tall. 'To survive,' he sighs; heads for the treeline.

To survive, survive, survive.

✢ ✢ ✢

I'd expected the banshee to return within days, but it took months. Months, and months; a black wolf on my front porch; a giant man on my couch; sharing food from the hunt. Somehow, nervous mistrust had evolved into quiet companionship. I learned he liked to touch. He learned I like to gift; a wooden wolf I'd carved from the old oak in my yard. I learned he loved the warmth. He learned I was always cold, hands like ice pressing to his chest. His name was Damien, name dripping from my tongue like sweet honey-
His visits involved far more clothing than our first rendezvous.
I tried not to be disappointed.
He seemed to know; a mischievous smirk curling the corners of his lips. He also seemed to know I wouldn't hurt him. Perhaps I thought the same of him.
Further visits had him losing the clothes.
A wailing in the night, so mournful and bone-shuddering it shakes me from my sleep. I'm on my feet in seconds; he's already half-shifted, dark fur growing from his cheeks and arms. 'It's

here.' He snarls; rolls from the bed.

I grab the rifle.

The lights flicker as I walk slowly, naked; bare, through the cabin. Breaths coming short, sharp; cold clouds misting before my lips. The wail comes again, closer this time. I feel ice in my veins. A warm nose is pressing into my back to urge me forward.

A chill spreads through the dark cabin, frost creeping over furniture and walls. The skittering of claws rattle behind me, wolf and dog close to each hip. It doesn't alleviate the visceral fear coursing through me.
'Alone,' Whispers a mournful, grief-filled voice; wet and raspy. 'Utterly and completely alone. Naught but the company of dogs and monsters. You destroyed them, Kahari- it's all you. Tore them apart from the inside out.'
The cold nose touches my arm. Encouraging. 'I'm not alone.' I announce to eerie silence. 'I did nothing. Death...' I hesitate; 'Death... is inevitable. Death happens to us all.'
'Too early, early... he despised you, in those gurgling last breaths. Your hesitation on the trigger was what killed him.'
'We were hunting a child,' I whisper, feeling the burn of tears in my eyes. She'd clawed Dad's throat out. I hadn't taken the shot. I didn't shoot.
'If you'd blown out her brains, he'd still be here. Come with me; come, come. My embrace is warm, and your family is here.'

Finally, I see it. The banshee. I see myself in its movements. Halting. Pained. Fatigued.
It drags itself across the floor toward me, dripping tar. I raise my rifle.

I don't shoot.

'You don't deserve to live. You don't deserve to be here. Do you think the wolf cares? He's waiting to rip your throat out the first chance that he gets. Just like the girl. Always a monster.'

'He's had every chance.' I breathe, teeth chattering so much I nearly bite my tongue. Damien rumbles deep in his chest. The banshee is nearly eye level. I lift the gun; the creature stares down the shaft.
'Pathetic.'

I shoot.

I take the veils away from the mirrors.

FLIGHT IN THE NIGHT

by Leola Rigg

My eyes snap open, senses on high alert. What woke me? I lie still, the remnants of a dream, in which something was here in my bunk with me, stroking me gently on the cheek, had intermingled momentarily with consciousness, but was already too translucent to grasp and study. I strain my eyes and ears for something amiss. There is no noise except the ocean, gurgling and babbling below, and the sailing gear creaking above. The cabin is in near darkness, moonlight fleetingly casts aside the shadows as the boat heels, caught in a momentary gust, then disappears, only the bronze porthole next to my bunk glints in reflected moonlight. Recalling with an accompanying prickle of rising hair on my exposed forearms that we are sailing through the Bermuda Triangle, I wonder if it was just the dream that woke me.

That day we had sailed the shallows of the Grand Bahama Bank, an eery experience - no land in sight yet the seabed a scant few meters down - our shadow accompanied us, sailing silently across the sandy seabed below, at one point a group of hammerheads lazily circled our vessel, sluggish in the light airs. Dad was unconcerned, he plotted our position on the chart in the same careful manner as always, while explaining the histories and mysteries of this area, nicknamed 'The devils triangle'. Inexplicable tales of disappeared ships and aircraft, in these very waters we ghost over now, pushed on by zephyrs that come and go, not the strong and steady blow of the trade winds we had come from. Of course, he hadn't meant to scare us, dad doesn't believe in ghosts and all that rubbish. I picture drowned sailors rising from their watery graves in Davy Jones locker to pass, spirit like into our boat; I slip out of bed, imagination getting the better of me. Standing for a moment in the centre of our tiny cabin, swaying to the gentle movement of the yacht, I peer into the dark passageway that leads to the saloon and wonder who is on watch – I hope it's dad, he doesn't mind if I sit on deck with him at night when we're sailing, mum thinks I'm going to magically fall overboard, just because I walked off the stern of the boat once while I was reading a book.

A sudden, surreal touch on my cheek makes me gasp and reflexively bring my hands up to grab the rotten flesh of long dead sailors trying to throttle me but there is nothing there, my hands grab thin air. Not caring who's on watch, I pad through the passage to the saloon, pausing at the bottom of the steep wooden companionway steps to see who is in the cockpit. It is dad, his bushy black beard and wavy hair are silhouetted by the moonlight behind him, so he looks like a lion with a huge shaggy mane. His presence calms me, like oil on a rough sea, and I reconsider the sensation I felt in the cabin, with a light breeze entering through the companionway, my long hair wafts at my face recreating a similar feeling, I must have imagined that touch, related to the dreams of myths and legends that woke me, surely. I won't say anything to dad, he'll think I'm being silly. I want to go on deck though, I love it on deck at night when we're cruising – have you ever seen a rainbow in the dark, a perfect, complete rainbow of different shades of grey, illuminated over a black ocean by the light of a full moon? I didn't know the moon could make rainbows like the sun, until I saw one. Dad hasn't noticed me yet, with one hand on the helm and the other on the main sheet, he is teasing more speed out of the yacht by trimming the mainsail to the fitful breezes that are constant in neither strength nor direction.

The sails glow luminously white against the night sky, billowing out over the dark water like giant spectres. I sit by dads' side at the helm, stars and planets stretch above us like a wizard's cloak. He points out the phosphorescence in our wake and tests me to find Polaris, which means identifying Ursula Major and following the pointers.

'Not tired?' Dad asks. 'Do you want to helm for a bit and I'll make some cocoa?'

'Yeah, ok'. What a treat! Dad was obviously fed up of teasing the wind that relentlessly teased him back.

'Steer by the stars,' he tells me, 'lights are all off except the nav lights to save energy, don't bother with the compass.'

I slide into his place behind the wheel, grasping the smooth, well-oiled spokes with both hands and choosing a star to steer her by, as he had taught me. The wheel could have been lashed for the few minutes needed to warm the milk, but he knows I like to helm. After a quick glance around the dark horizon, he disappears below decks and a moment later the small, fluorescent galley light flickers on and I smell the distinct gassy vapour that always accompanies lighting the stove. I look out to sea, the unsteady breeze means the sails sometimes hang slack, then fill with a crack when the wind returns, it is a frustrating condition to sail in and alone on deck, my thoughts turn again to the long dead below us, I worry we are not going fast enough to out sail those trying to escape Davy Jones locker, or perhaps wanting to drag a small child down with them; perhaps dad would return in a minute and I would no longer be here, but down there, rotten salt-encrusted fingers round my neck, because we are dragging our heels across this infamous stretch of ocean. I lash the helm with the short lines port and starboard to hold the wheel in place, I'll go down and be with dad, offer to help bring the cups up so he doesn't know I'm scared. A sudden, high pitched shriek from below deck startles me and I stop mid-way across the cockpit – what was that?

'Dad?' I call quietly.

'What was that?' He echoes my thought, a slight wobble in his usually dead pan voice.

I start down the companionway, just as he turns the main saloon light on. The boat herself seems to come alive, the bulkheads all around us vibrate and convulse, the deckhead seems to be falling in, I stand, a scream preparing itself in my throat. Dad beats me to it, screeching and flapping his arms about, he sounds like an idiotic schoolgirl being sprayed by a water gun and pretending it's the end of the world. The thing that seemed to shed like an alien skin from the boat as dad put the main light on, is now separating into a million pairs of crazed wings as a stampede of vastly diverse moths go crazy over the light, slowly being extinguished by a fluttering, flittering, flapping mass. I stare at them in amazement, some are enormous, at least as big as both of my hands put together, they crawl across the white bulkheads of the saloon, dusty wings folded up to show off grotesquely furry bodies and long, bent legs – they remind me of those evil flying creatures from Jason and the Argonauts and I kind of see why dad is freaking out. He has grabbed a spatula from the galley and is swatting them viciously against the sides of the boat, the moths seem invincible though and flutter away, only a dusty silver imprint left behind. Mum tumbles out of bed and bangs her head on the low passageway through to the saloon, pulling on her red checked dressing gown and cursing; she comes to create order, as always.

'Michael,' she demands, then stops dead as she enters the light, mouth open, speechless.

My brother crashes into her from behind and they both spill out into the fluttering bodies. Dad returns to swatting moths, war shouts and girlish cries spill from his mouth, he starts to swing the spatula through the moth filled air, connecting with tens of bodies that ricochet across the boat. Mum, having just woken up to discover her home full of moths and her husband gone utterly mad, in the middle of the ocean, takes control.

'Outside, now.' She snaps at him, grabs the spatula from his hand and threatens him with it until he disappears up the companionway.

We assess the situation. Where did they all came from? It is reminiscent of the 'The Birds' by Alfred Hitchcock, only with moths instead. Mum stands calm amidst the furious flurry of activity in the air all around us, thinking. She turns all lights off except in the heads, hoping the moths migrate there. It seems to be working and we sit on deck together, while below the air is filled with fluttering wings, as like fairies in the night, they dance towards the glow. We go down and peek into the heads, it is an awesome sight, every inch of surface is covered in moths, crawling over each other and flapping feebly, fighting over the one light, faint beneath a sea of bodies and wings. We open the porthole and close the door so they can only escape over the side of the boat. Feeling as though we have all shared the same bizarre dream, one that will dissipate in the daylight as though scared of the sun, we return to our bunks. Another mystery of the 'Devils Triangle'.

HORSING AROUND IN FALKIRK

by Amy Cornock

'Daddy, it's a climbing frame,' exclaims a wee boy horsing around on his neon blue Raleigh bike. An image of Jack and the Beanstalk randomly springs to mind. When I was a child a galvanised climbing dome seemed as high as Ben Nevis, something I dreamed to climb to the top of one day. But for today's generation, only a 100-foot sculpture will suffice.

I treat myself to a cappuccino from the Horsebox café which warms my bones on this rather 'dreich' Saturday afternoon. The Kelpies rise out of the dappled sky, the energy shines out of them like the sun trying to escape the clouds. They're comprised of 464 steel sheet panels which fit into place like a jigsaw; the bolts which join them add strength of character. The cacophony of birds singing inside them gives these creatures a voice. There is a sense of tension between them, one has their head lowered, gazing down on me with a steely look in his eyes and the other head is strained and points towards the sky. His ears are raised, like a flower bud coming to life, so graceful yet powerful.

When asked what the inspiration was behind this project, sculptor Andy Scott replied,

'I took the title the client gave me but steered towards the heritage of working horses and the industries of central Scotland rather than the mythological inspirations of the traditional Kelpies.'

Duke and Baron were two Scottish born and bred working Clydesdale horses who the Kelpies were modelled on. As they were the world's largest breed of horse, Clydesdales were used to tow barges and plough the land and were a driving force in industry during the industrial revolution.

As I lift my head from my compostable coffee cup I see freshly painted barges in the distance waiting patiently to sail down the Forth & Clyde canal while stallions graze in the neighbouring fields. I almost feel like I've been transported back in time if it weren't for the sounds of the cars whizzing down the M9.

An elderly couple greet two teenagers with a cheery 'afternoon.' The selfie ready girls smile back as they pose on the steps between both structures; no doubt this would be their new Instagram profile pic within seconds.

When asked what the Kelpies mean to Andy personally, he replied, 'I'm very proud of them now, of how they've become national and hugely popular icons. It has taken considerable time and distance to be able to reflect on the achievement with pride. We all achieved something truly amazing there and I don't think it will be repeated in Scotland in my lifetime.'

I throw a penny into the murky water which surrounds them while making a wish, emotion takes hold as I bid farewell. As it gets dark, their heads light up. Bright red beams out of every crevice. The skyline once synonymous with the fires of the nearby BP oil refinery has been transformed by the world's largest equine sculptures.

TWIRLING IN THE WIND

by Christopher Beames

They were lucky they didn't live in a flat. Steve's footsteps were not the only things making more noise than they really should. She knew exactly where he was and what he was doing the entire argument.

'Say something!' he said, looking at her from across the lounge.

'What do you want me to say?' she replied, looking at him from the kitchen doorway with her arms crossed.

'Anything. I'm leaving Karen, I'm going, look' he raised a duffle bag.

'Yes, I can see that.'

'And that's all you're gonna to say?'

'I don't know what to say' she shrugged.

'Bye Karen.' The final slam followed his exit.

The clock still read quarter to. Most of the office was empty now, there were very few people who would stay till the absolute end of the workday, some even stayed later. Leaving at exactly five o'clock meant heading straight into traffic. Karen's friend Aubrey had put on her coat and was headed to Karen's desk. Karen only noticed because for a second a purple full-length coat obscured the clock.

'Let's go,' said Aubrey. Karen was still looking at the clock. 'Karen? Karen?' she waved a hand in front of Karen's face.

'Oh, yeah, nearly, 15 minutes'.

'Pff as if, what's up with you?'

'Me? Oh, nothing'

'Behave, c'mon, you can tell Aunty Aubrey all about it on the way to the car park'.

Karen was still staring at the clock, her eyes wider than an open mouth. Aubrey wondered if at this point someone else was meant to take over from Karen's tear ducts, who look to have been so overworked, they have completely given up. She could chuck water in Karen's face, or perhaps pinch her eyes closed temporarily. She decided, instead, to touch her on the shoulder.

'Karen, let's go for a little walk'.

'hm? OK'.

PING. The elevator arrived at their floor. Aubrey waited for Karen to notice. Karen was still looking widely at nothing very much. Aubrey gave her a guiding nudge towards the lift. They stood next to one another but said nothing, Aubrey rocked on her feet looking at everything but Karen. The hum of the elevator gears was clear over the silence of the elevator car. Aubrey pressed the emergency stop button.

'What are you doing?'

'Worrying about you.'

'What? Why? Let's just go.'

'You've been like this for weeks, please talk to me.'

'There's nothing more to say'

'What has the doctor said?'

'I don't want to talk about it.'

'Karen.'

'Aubrey.'

'Have you spoken to Steve?'

'Let it go.'

Aubrey released the button and the elevator continued. The doors opened to the cold car park. Aubrey opened her arms to Karen who stood in close but made very little effort to raise her arms back. Aubrey felt like she was hugging her fourteen-year-old nephew.

'See you tomorrow?' Aubrey asked with eyes wide, and

eyebrows raised.

'MM hmm, see ya.' Karen barely looked back as she replied, headed already to her car.

"Quarter to and quarter past" her instructor would always say. He was a nice man, she passed first time. He was called Mr. Fredrickson and when she passed, he was called Dennis. There was never any reason not to have both her hands on the wheel. She loved learning to drive, they would go three times a week and she had passed within two months. Dennis loved to talk about musicals. Especially from the west end. Some lessons, if the roads were quiet enough, they would both sing along to Wicked. She wished she could defy gravity now. The traffic seemed to stretch on forever and the lane out the window going the other way seemed clear, open, and free. The occasional coloured blur would fly past and away.

'We are going to be late!' Said Steve as he wrapped his knuckles on the table.

'We have loads of time, you made sure of that.'

'This is why,' he gestured at Karen as though he was presenting her as evidence, 'Please hurry up, I don't want to have to find our seats while the people behind us are trying to enjoy the show.'

'Find our seats, ha, you know exactly where our seats are.'

'Can you just?'

'Alright, alright, let me just finish this, it's not like you've never seen Annie before.'

'We. Do. Not. Have. Time.'

'Course we do, it's just an ice cream'.

'Just an ice cream?? That's bigger than your head'.

'Then we are agreed: too much to waste.'

'Fine. Where's a spoon?'

'That's the spirit' she produced a spoon as though from a holster.

'What's this?' his spoon hit something hard in the sundae bowl.

'Ooo I don't know, why don't you have a look?' She smiled.

'Karen?... Really?' He held a piece of rock candy with the word pregnant written in the core.

'Really.'

'How long have you known?' He nearly threw the table with his legs as he stood up.

'I didn't get my period for two months. It took two weeks for the candy to be delivered. Then I just had to wait for a musical... so not long after that.'

'Shut up' he smiled poking her face with the flat end of the rock.

She flicked through the radio stations, disconnected words from disembodied voices mashed together as she struggled to find a program. She liked driving with company. Whenever her family went on holiday, they took the car. Dad loved driving even though ninety percent of the time he would protest that he didn't. The seat was never right, the radio always the wrong volume and don't get him started on other drivers. But he had driving gloves and mum bought him an apron one Christmas that said, 'Ask me about my Mazda'. He rarely drives at all now, but when he does, it's in his Mazda.

'Where am I taking you?'

'The pub' Karen rolled her eyes.

'OK well, put your seat belt on, you never know the sort of idiots that are going to be on the road.' He put his hand on her chair as he reversed off the drive.

'Yes Dad, well, we know you are on the road' she paused for a second to enjoy his reaction, but he was old now and only gave her a sideways glance.

'Which pub?'

'Any.'

'Any? You going on your own?'

'No silly, I'm going with you.'

'Well, I can't go to the pub if I'm driving.'

'And I can't go to the pub if I'm pregnant'.
'Kitkat'
'Dad'
'Oh you muppet, let me pull over.'
'Dad, are you crying?'
'Of course I am!'

She tapped on the steering wheel. Rain tapped the windscreen. She turned the wipers on. Traffic was still barely moving. A red car in front of hers stopped all together and a tiny hand was reaching out into the weather. Red had always been her favourite colour, her Mum's too. There are baby pictures of them both wearing a little red bow. You can't get the bows anymore; they were made in Sweden by a man who handmade doll clothes. They fit babies perfectly.

'Hello fatty!' called Steve.
'Thanks for that - have you got the ice cream?' said Karen climbing down from the step ladder.
'Of course, you think I'd risk not feeding the beast?'
'Oh shut up and give it here.'
'That's for you' he pulled his hand back after she had taken the tub and spoon.
'Har har' she said while shaking her head and tearing the lid from the ice cream pot.
'Wow, look at the progress' he said surveying the room with his hands on his hips.
'You like it?' said Karen while accidentally wiping her forehead with red paint.
'Like it? I love it. What a perfect tribute to your mother.'
'I just wish we still had the bow.'
'A bow painting is still a bow.'
'Thanks, Steve.'
'And, a bow is still a bow' he held out his left hand and put his right arm around her.
'Steve! Where did you find this?'

'eBay, collection only, I wasn't really in Magaluf.'

'Oh, well, that makes sense.'

'Yeah, can you imagine? Surprised you bought that to tell you the truth. This is from a collector in Aberdeen, they wanted to make sure it was going to someone who would love it as much as they did.'

'Oh Stevie, of course we will' she kissed him on the cheek with ice cold lips.

A car beeps loudly behind her. The traffic has begun to shuffle forwards. They move now just as much as they stop. Move, stop, move, stop. Like the steady beat of a drum. On, off, on, off.

'Her hands are so cold'

Beep.

'She looks so small'

Beep.

'She looks so peaceful'

Beep.

'Perhaps she is'

Beep.

'The doctor said we can be here as long as we want.'

Beep.

Beep Beep. Beeep. The traffic had begun to move more steadily. The clouds were getting darker by the minute and on the not-too-distant horizon flashes foretold of cracks soon to come. She hated thunder and lighting. The summertime was always her favourite. She could wear long dresses that were lifted by the wind and the trees were always bushy and full, in that way that small children sometimes have long free hair. There was a shop in town that she and her mother went to semi-religiously to get ice cream called 'Mr. Whatty'. When she was younger her mother would make her order her own ice cream knowing full well what would happen.

'Mr. Whippy please' Karen would say.

'Nearly, it's Mr. Whatty' the shopkeeper would reply.

She would sigh and go red while her mother and the shopkeeper would have a good laugh at her expense. The ice creams there were the best though, so she didn't mind. The shopkeeper doesn't try to pull her leg anymore.

'What will you have today Mum?'

'Oh, there is so much that I would love to have again.'

'Alright Mum, we are here every year' Karen said with a raised eyebrow.

'Yes. Yes I'll have the 'Salted Caramel Captain''

'With chocolate pirate hat?' asked Mr. Whatty.

'Why not.' Answered Mum.

'Ooo pushing the boat out today?' Karen handed the money to Mr. Whatty.

'You could say that.'

They sat where they always sat, next to the aviary. There was an art gallery nearby. They liked to walk around and laugh at and the birds who sometimes sung rude words.

'So? What are we celebrating?'

'The end of a long career'

'You retired years ago, what's with you today?'

'I know sweetie, I wish there were an easy way to tell you.'

'Mum, tell me what? You're scaring me.'

'Oh Kit Kat, I'm scared too' she rested her hand on Karen's knee.

'Mum?'

'Karen, I'm dying.'

'What do you mean you're dying?

'Cancer, stage three'

She approached a roundabout and although she was driving a familiar route, she found herself in the presence of a brand-new choice. There were three exits. The first lead back home, to her life as it is now. The second to the hospital, to her life as it might be. The third, and final choice, a way she had never been. She made her way onto the roundabout. She and Steve used to like trying new things together. Karate was one of her favourites, but Steve hated being beaten by a girl.

'Would you like a taste?'

'Huh?'

'Of the sauce. Chermoula' he said with an exaggerated "la".

'Oh. Nah.'

'C'mon, it's Moroccan.'

'Ok' said Karen verbalising a shrug.

'Remember Morocco? We went because you thought it was Greece.'

'No, I didn't'

'Yes, you did! We went to Morocco because you said that's where they filmed Mamma Mia.'

'So I didn't think it was Greece.'

'Are you OK?' He stopped stirring the Chermoula.

'You know I'm not.'

'Are you going to talk to me?'

'I am'

'You know what I mean, Karen.'

'You aren't speaking French.'

'Well then? How long am I going to be hitting my head against this wall?'

'I'm so empty, Steve.'

'What did the doctor say?'

'Just leave me alone, OK?'

'OK,' he sighed and went back to the cooking.

Her phone rang and she hit ignore. Thunder cracked. The road stretched into the horizon and around the cliff-top. The raging storm overhead had cleared the road down below. She was alone. She hated to be alone. When she was young her parents seemed to have all the time in the world just to play hide and seek and guessing games.

'Thanks for coming in, I appreciate this a difficult time, so I'll try to get to the point.'

'OK?'

'OK so, miscarriages are really quite common and often they are nothing to worry about' her ears stood up like a dog who's heard the word walk 'but there are certain conditions which can impact a pregnancy and looking through your family history…'

All the oxygen seemed to leave the room and the doctors' voice barely made it through the ringing and the memory of her mother's voice saying:

'Cancer. Stage three.'

The doctor called again, and she let the ring tone continue. She saw the ocean under the cliff edge and the road turn away. She put her foot down a little more. The tempestuous dark grey sea matching the thunderous sky. All-consuming chaos, a never-ending distraction.

THE FALLING

by Verity Kane

'What's going off? Fuck, are you ok? Matt? Talk to me.' I watched as my husband took off a belt of grenades and magazine clips, dropped them on the kitchen table, next to his pistol and SA80 rifle. He'd just come in from his first night back at work.

'Nicole, I'm tired and I need a shower, my dhobi done, some scran and a kip before I go back on stag in a couple of hours.'

'But what's with all the stuff? And the news? There's so much bad shit on the news. What's happened?'

Matt smiled at me and simply said 'this is standard out here babe. We always carry this shit, and you don't see half of what goes on over here on the box at home.' If it hadn't been for that reassuring smile, the smile I fell in love with and married just over a week ago, I'd have packed my bags and gone home to my mother in Swansea.

We met when he'd come home from London for a weekend a year previously. He was handsome in his shirt, chinos and dessert boot "out of barracks uniform", with a sandy tan from a recent exercise in Kenya.

We'd spent our weeklong "honeymoon" packing up my stuff and saying goodbye to friends and family and at just twenty years old I found myself travelling to our new home for the next two years, a married quarter in Shackleton Barracks, just outside Limavady, Northern Ireland.

'I'll be ok though, won't I?' My crucifix was cold on my clavicle.

We were on the way to our new home and Matt looked over at me. It was certainly a wakeup call for me. Back home we only heard about bomb threats occasionally, here it was a daily occurrence and the first thing I'd seen on the early morning news.

'I'd take that off if I were you. You might think being a Catholic is a good thing. It's not. You're a traitor in their eyes.' Harsh words to hear. 'Sorry Nicole.'

Barely two months had passed and those conversations already felt a lifetime away. It was late November and only a week earlier the IRA had bombed the town centre in Coleraine, just up the road; fortunately nobody was injured and sadly I was already becoming oblivious. We were now sat outside the ferry terminal in Belfast, collecting both our mothers who were visiting pre-Christmas and to presumably judge my home-making skills.

'It'll be fine Nic, don't worry,' that reassuring smile again, that flutter in my chest.

After the usual bustle of bags in the boot, hugs on the kerbside and the who-sits-in-the-front argument we were on the way back through the city centre. The mums were tittering away in the back getting louder whilst I became more nervous about hosting them for five whole days. Matt's hand was warm on my knee, and I took comfort from that. We'd driven east and then south so that our mothers could see some of the city, before heading north again, which was ridiculous really because we'd been so close to the A6 to get out of the city quickly.

Matt's hand jumped from my knee to the steering wheel. He was tense, and I suddenly understood what people meant when they said the atmosphere could thicken enough to be cut.

'They're just excited, don't let them put you off.' It was difficult enough to concentrate in a busy city at rush hour on a Friday, he probably didn't need them distracting him too.

'Shut up.'

'Excuse me?' Trying to keep it down I wanted to let him know that he couldn't speak to me that way.

'Just shut up will you.'

My chest hurt a little. This wasn't Matt's usual style. Even from the passenger side I could feel his hands tighten on the steering wheel. Something was wrong.

'Fuck. Fuck.' Then more loudly, 'Mum, Aileen? Can you just be quiet a minute please?'

'We're just having a laugh, Matt! Don't let us put you off.' And directed at my mother 'I've always said men can't multi-task.' More tittering.

'Seriously, shut up mother.'

I cringed. That would hurt. Matt was her only child, and they'd waited a long time to have him, then nearly lost him to pneumonia when he was 6. She doted on him, and he adored her in return. I was starting to feel sick, and I didn't understand why. Matt was anxiously looking in his rear-view mirror every couple of seconds and I started to work out was wrong.

'I've taken a wrong turn Nic.' I balked. I didn't know much, but I knew Belfast was split and there were areas we were welcome in and areas we weren't.

'Matt… Where, where are we?'

'Nic, please don't.'

'Seriously, where are we?'

'The Falls Road.'

'Shit.' I glanced at the wing mirror and could see my mother straining to hear the conversation going on in the front. The initial nausea was threatening to become much more physical. Only four years ago two British Army Corporals had inadvertently stumbled across an IRA funeral; they'd been captured, dragged from their car and torn apart like prey.

'Can't you just go back? We've only just turned on here.'

'Are you fucking kidding me Nic? If I stop this car now and turn around every man and his dog will know we're lost, and believe you me, they're watching us.' I stole a look at the net curtains covering the windows of the terraced houses. 'Look at me. Look at how I'm dressed, look at my hair cut. It's fucking obvious who I am, even in civvies.'

It was too late. A tear hit my top lip. I raised my hand to my face and leant my elbow on the door, hoping to look bored and not terrified.

'Jesus, this place is gopping. We need to bug out as soon as. But not too soon. I need to do this in a way that isn't fucking obvious Nic. Nic, I'm sorry.'

'It's ok. Really. It's not your fault. You know I love you right?' I wasn't sure if it was my imagination or if the street was getting busier. There seemed to be a lot of people stood on their front doorsteps, given the late November temperature. It was getting dark, and I hoped this would be a good thing. The darker it was the less likely they could see Matt's squaddie haircut and civvy uniform of button-down collar. The cold metal on my clavicle felt heavy and burned like ice. I should have listened to him, I should have taken it off, but it was my nan's and was sentimental as well as a symbol of my faith. Bollocks, when would I learn to listen to other people's advice?

'I'm gonna get beasted for this mother fucking mistake.' The self-loathing was obvious.

'Do you have to tell them?'

'Shit, yes. They'll have my number plate now, I'll need to get it changed.'

'Are we turning off yet? We've passed a couple of roads.'

'Yes, but I can't turn off too soon, that's like turning around and going back. Besides, I only looked at the map briefly, I don't know where those roads go. They might be dead ends with the signs taken down. I'm not getting fucking ambushed with my wife and our mothers in the car for fucks sake.'

That was nearly 30 years ago now. I can still feel it. The crucifix ripped from my neck, the coldness of the metal leaving the warmth of my throat. I can still hear it. Our mothers, screaming in the back seat as we were torn from the front. I hope they didn't feel it like I did. I hope they died quickly. Matt somehow managed to struggle free, clambering over the bonnet to me, covering me with his body, taking the blows, trying to protect me.

The last thing I remember is my mother telling me how much she loved me. She looked me in the eye. Called me her baby as she was dragged from the broken window. She reached out her hand to me, our fingers touching momentarily, fleetingly sharing the electric connection of child and parent. Matt laid on top of me, shaking, crying, apologising. Aileen's voice somewhere far away, calling out for her son. I just hope they all knew the love I had for them. The brick came down on mum's head. Like a hammer on a church bell tolling midday. I don't know if it only took the one blow. I don't like to think about it.

Bloody and dusty, the brick was soon closer than I thought. The pain between my eyes was excruciating. Matt's scream was blood-curdling. They were keeping him alive to watch the demise of his loved one's. I didn't know much, but I knew how this worked.

I just hope one day I'll be allowed to be dead in peace. That they'll finally find the last pieces of my body and lay them to rest with the pieces of my husband.

LIFE

by Kimberley Deer

Elizabeth held her breath as she walked through the door. The too-strong smell of bleach made her head ache. The echoes of her squeaking boots bounced off the shiny floors and multiplied up the beige walls before coming back to her sensitive ears. She shuddered; the sound of approaching feet had always meant trouble when she was inside. She glanced at the mauve curtains framing the single-glazed windows. This had been a hotel before it was converted into a residential home. The main foyer featured manifold, uninspiring artworks. They were all nature scenes, rainbows, and rivers that would have been dazzling if they hadn't all been rendered in solemn sepia tones. She rang the service bell with its polite ting! It was odd, that they should still have such an old-fashioned bell when the beep and hum of modern medical equipment was loud enough to overshadow the cheery radio on the reception desk.

'I'm here to see my mother - Mrs Doe.'

'We didn't think she had any relatives.'

'Could you give me her room number?'

'She's in room 105, third floor on the left. You won't be able to take those in. Infection control.' Elizabeth looked down at the flowers in her hand. They were divine. A gorgeous bunch of cerise

Stargazer lilies. Their elegant, emerald stems supported a host of voluptuous fuchsia petals. The orange pollen coating the protruding stamens was poisonous to cats and dogs. To humans too, but not enough to kill them. There were other plants for that.

'I've spent a lot of money on these flowers, I'll be taking them in.'

'It's against the rules.'

'Then the rules are fucking wrong.' Elizabeth hadn't raised her voice. If anything, she'd spoken more quietly than before. But the hand wrapped around the flowers was shaking and the tendons stood proudly in the side of her neck. She made direct eye contact with the receptionist for a few moments until the other woman looked down. Then she turned slowly towards the lift carrying her illicit bouquet.

The elevator was situated next to a grand staircase. Its ornate oak bannister was covered in intricate filigree that had faded almost beyond recognition. She would take the stairs. She had no intention of going in a lift for the rest of her life. She'd had more than enough of grey spaces with no windows.

Her black, sturdy footwear disturbed dust motes from the khaki carpet; it was the mottled combination of greens vaguely reminiscent of a forest floor. Phony foliage to complement the plastic plants strategically arranged on each landing. She stopped to touch one, sliding her fingers along the edge of a never-living, polymerised Peace Lily. It had no smell, strange when everything else here smelt of decay.

It was difficult to make out door numbers in the weak offering of a single strip light. She was on the third floor. Somehow the journey had been longer than expected. Fifteen years longer. Elizabeth strode silently along the corridor. She turned left, straight into the reflection of a gold, bevel-edged mirror that dominated the hallway. She grimaced as she examined her diminutive figure. The poor illumination exaggerated the puffy bags under her eyes. The streaks of white creeping prematurely into her otherwise raven hair.

The flowers she carried seemed to mock her with their exorbitant display of colour. She frowned at them. How easy it would be to snap their fragile necks. One by one. But they were her mother's favourites. She carried on walking, past what must have been the hotel ballroom. The rich, red swag curtains draped onto the chestnut parquet dancefloor. A couple of residents waltzed along to a crackling record that was spinning seventy-eight rounds per minute on an old grammar phone. They laughed and hugged and smiled at each other. Genuine smiles; not the bared-teeth grin of a wolf assessing a new-born lamb.

She hurried on. Faster now, down the homogenous corridors. Peering left to right at the embossed digits on the peeling entrances. She wondered briefly what kind of people lived in those rooms. Did they choose to be here? Was it convenient for them, close to family perhaps? Or was it all they could afford? She was getting closer, room 103,104. Here. Her heart beat in jagged synchronicity with her fist as she knocked on the door. One, two, three times. She waited. Could she hear something? It was impossible to tell over the cacophonous surge of blood preparing her body to run or to fight. She reached for the door handle. It was a burnished bronze oval, you could still smell the polish.

Elizabeth pushed the door open but didn't cross the threshold. On the wall opposite the door hung a large crucifix. She couldn't meet the baleful eyes crying crimson tears down the wooden cross. She hesitated, caught in that liminal space like a vampire waiting to be invited in.

'Mum?' A woman sat, small in a straight-backed dun-coloured

armchair. The room was Spartan. There was no comfort here. The few items present were generic, impersonal. A cream bedspread adorned a pine bed frame. A commode loitered in the corner as if it was embarrassed to be there. Various bibles and hymn books were stacked neatly on a set of utilitarian shelves, they were alphabetised, all present and correct. No fiction and definitely no crime. The blank canvas of the magnolia walls made the silver gilt picture frame all the more conspicuous. Elaborate hearts and curlicues encircled the image of a woman hugging a grinning man. All of the man's teeth were showing. The woman was wearing too much make-up. Along the edge of her jaw you could just make out the creeping tendril of a purple bruise. The tarnished photo had been torn and painstakingly repaired until the damage was barely visible.

'Are you one of my new nurses?'

'No mum, it's me, Lizzy.' The cross around her mother's neck glinted. It was as pristine as the day she had bought it for her. Elizabeth remembered taking money out of the church collection dish to buy it. Just a few dollars here and there.

'I don't know any Lizzy. My nurse's name is Tabitha. Have you worked here long?'

'I don't work here mum, I'm your daughter, Elizabeth. I brought flowers.' She looked briefly for a vase, but there was nothing here. Only him in that damned picture. Only him, and her mother, and God. Just like it had always been. Her mother's confused gaze held no recognition. Elizabeth inched into the room, she laid the flowers down onto the smooth wood of the desk near the door. She knelt close to her mother's face.

'They told me your memory wasn't good mum. That's why I was allowed to come here. To see you one last time. I kept thinking you would visit me or write me a letter. I used to pray for that.' Her mother's grip tightened on the chair.

'You have no right to pray for anything!' she hissed, 'You tore this family apart. What you did can never be forgiven. Never.' The tears ran silently down Elizabeth's face. She didn't make any noise, she knew not to draw attention to herself.

'Isn't your God all about forgiveness mum?' Her mother clutched at the cross around her neck, rocking back and forth on the chair.

'Oh God, deliver me from my enemies,' she stammered, 'deliver me from evildoers. He was your father Lizzy, your own father.'

'I know. That only makes it worse how he treated you. He would have killed you eventually. That knife cut straight through his bullshit. Such a small blade to expose such a big lie.' Her mother was crying as well now. Great, gasping sobs that ripped themselves free of her chest.

'Why have you come here? Are you finally going to say sorry?'

'I am sorry mum. Sorry that you were caught up in this. Sorry that you've ended up in this shithole. I know you were just as afraid as I was.'

'Get out. I don't have to listen to your vitriol.'

'I love you mum, I wish you could love me too.'

'Get out and take those flowers with you.' A blue-clad nurse had appeared in the doorway.

'Are you alright Mrs Doe? The couple next door rang down to say they could hear shouting in here.'

'Tabitha, you've got to make her leave. She's a criminal. She snuck in here to kill me. She'll poison my food so I can't struggle. She looks so small but she's malicious.' The nurse pulled a small bottle inscribed 'Donepezil' from her pocket.

'It's alright Mrs Doe, there's no need to be upset, I think you're a bit late taking your medication tonight. How about we give you something to help you sleep as well?' The nurse turned to Elizabeth,

'I think it's better if you leave her now sorry. She gets very confused later in the evening.'

'You don't need to apologise for her. I know it's not her fault.' Elizabeth stood. She collected the flowers. They were already drooping. The lack of water and sunlight had robbed them of their vitality. 'I wish I could have come more often.'

'Is this your friend Tabitha? Why isn't she wearing a nurse's uniform? Just started here I expect.' Elizabeth looked back at what was left of her mother. The tears had gone now, evaporated along with the history they had once shared. She walked back the way she had come. Down the corridor, turn right. Past the mirror and through the jungle of fake flora. Music drifted toward her from the old ballroom. It pulled her inexorably onwards, through the glass doors. She jumped when the stylus lifted off the clicking record and swung itself gracefully up and over onto its waiting bracket. The couple had already chosen their next song and set it tenderly spinning. She didn't recognise it but the melody was smooth and repetitive. The man smiled. He asked softly,

'Come to visit your parents, is it? Those flowers are beautiful. We're not allowed them in here. Infection control. Me and my Viv have been doing a roaring trade in succulents for the last few years. Easy to keep them going indoors you see.'

'I was visiting my mother, but I won't be able to come again.'

'It's not so bad here, sure the building needs a freshen up but you wouldn't get a ballroom like this anywhere else. We were champions in our day, "The Magnificent Marlon and Vivien." We even had a sprung floor fitted in our old house. Then Viv started forgetting things. She'd wander outside in the nights. In the end, I had to lock the doors like a prison.' Elizabeth felt the tears welling. 'I'm sorry, I didn't mean to upset you. Here, let me show you some moves.' The man spun her around with surprising agility and went to slip her coat off her shoulders.

'No!' She wrenched the jacket back. It was too late. She heard him gasp as his hazel eyes absorbed the shock. She felt the caress of the warm Texan breeze exploring the scars that bisected her back at every angle. Fifty lashes her father had inflicted on her for stealing that collection money. He'd never told her mother why he'd done it. Elizabeth had seen him wrapping the silver cross. She'd stayed silent when he'd presented it to her mother and she'd said it was the best gift he'd ever gotten her.

She'd been fifteen at the time. It was only a month later that she'd enrolled as a Private. It had been on her second tour of Afghanistan that she'd found them. There had been rumours and red herrings but finally she'd got the real thing. She'd been patient, disciplined when her tour ended and she'd come home. She'd cultivated the trumpet-shaped yellow flowers in her room under an overpriced hydroponic light system. Two hundred and forty watts with eighty percent humidity. She'd never forget the formula. When they'd finally flowered they looked like little buttercups and their waxy leaves were tasteless. He was a big man, it had taken several doses before the diarrhoea and depression had disabled him. Her mother had run upstairs to pack a bag for the hospital.

'Where's that useless bitch gone?' he'd spat. 'I'll be out later tonight. What's she packing a bag for?'

He'd gripped Elizabeth's wrist. His fingers encircled it easily. 'I know you had something to do with this. I saw those fucking flowers in your room. Never been green-fingered before. Light fingered maybe.' He snorted at his own joke. 'Maybe not even fifty lashes will be enough for this girl. Maybe fifty for your mother as well.' His grip had tightened on her arm. What if he was right? What if they didn't keep him in? His hand had constricted her. He was going to break her wrist. She'd felt the bones grating together. How was this happening again? A steak knife had still been on the table from his dinner. She'd picked it up.

'Let me go.'

'Think you're strong now with all your medals, soldier girl? You'll never be stronger than me.' The knife had punctuated his sentence with a full stop. She'd heard the footsteps and the thud as the suitcase hit the floor. Her mother's screams still ricochet through her memory, a discordant harmony to her father's rattling groans.

Marlon cleared his throat, bringing her back to the living. Elizabeth shrugged the jacket back onto her shoulders.

'I'm sorry I shouted at you, Marlon. Please give these flowers to Viv, I can't take them with me.' He hesitated, then gently accepted them.

'God bless you,' he whispered. Elizabeth sighed. She walked down the stairs and back through the foyer. The receptionist had made herself scarce. Outside they were waiting to put her handcuffs back on. They tightened them until the metal cut the skin. Four armed officers escorted her at all times. She'd been a PR nightmare, war hero turned murderer. They shoved her into the back of the police car. No one looked at her. No one spoke. The glowing orb of the moon bathed the streets. She tried to look out of the car window but they pushed her roughly away. It didn't go down well, killing a priest. Pre-meditated murder. Life.

LAND AHOY

by Leola Rigg

The first time I was forced to live on solid ground, it closed about me like a dizzying maze, I became the Minotaur, gifted from Poseidon, and all land the labyrinth imprisoning me. From north, east, south, west and every point between rose unmoving giants blocking out my horizon, hard tarmac streets froze below me into rivers of black ice; I moved like an ever-drunken sailor, swaying to a rhythm surging only within me. Living on land became a night that progressively deepened until the darkness suffocated my soul and strangled my spirit.

So when my daughter, grown as tall and proud as the dusky pink nipples she once fiercely suckled, held me hostage with her dark, heavily lashed eyes, the only part of her face not a replica of my own, and said:

'Mum, I want to live on land, in a house, like normal people.'

My heart stopped, rising to my throat to gag me and stifle the scream I couldn't let reverberate around the cliffs like a beached whale in distress. It wasn't the first time, but until then I had succeeded in letting the words slide from me like the ocean through my wide scuppers in a rolling storm. I had no desire, then, to be normal, but I could see the truth in her eyes and hear the plea poured forth. And, I could remember a time when I did want to be normal. Her words brought memories surging back that I had successfully kept below the surface for many years, they sunk me to the unfathomable depths of the Marianna Trench where the blackness was tangible and the cold like a wetted knife, somewhere so deep beneath that shimmering, undulating line between one world and another I thought I may never break the surface again. Immense pressure squeezed into me turning my guts to jelly and my brain to gloop. A sense of foreboding overflowed within me; hurricane force winds that split the steering cable mid-Atlantic with a terrifying twanging and left the boat rolling like a pig in muck between endless towering mountains, marching and roaring, frothing at the mouth and spitting salty spray in my eyes, had not created such a sinking feeling.

Somehow, like a fish, a swim bladder inflated internally, buoying me back up to the glorious ocean surface once more, where the sun was warm and bright and the faces of my children looked down expectantly, each offering a hand to pull me from the ocean's embrace, and hold me tight as I wept. When the new owners stepped aboard, I let go of the helm, my business, my way of life, and another home I loved so strongly. I swilled a bucket of salty tears over her decks as my final goodbye.

I read a poem the other day, it didn't enthral me, didn't call out to be learnt by heart and repeated in times of need, it just resonated. The first line was 'They fuck you up, your mum and dad'. I find it a revelation when I come across my own thoughts, written plainly by another for all the world to see. It made me stop and think, of the past, the future, of my own children; because it was for this, in an effort not to fuck them up, that I capsized my own life, my children were the rogue waves that rocked my boat but also the buoyancy aids that stopped me drowning. Growing up, I had no say in life changing decisions, they just happened, maybe that's how it should be, but I can remember a fierce, burning hate for my own parents, a fingered blame that said everything that happened to me on land the first time was their fault.

As a child, the open ocean, that enormous globe-spanning entity that offers a 360 degree horizon and an extra dimensional life where the very surface upon which you live is never still, never silent, always changing, coming alive; was my country, and my home a sailing spray called Jumbly Girl. The first taste I remember on my tongue is the ocean's salt tang, the first sight to enthral me was that immense dynamic window into another world. The ocean's swell and its perpetual gurgling babble below our hull rocked and sung me to sleep since the day I was born. The skyscrapers of my city the tall masts that swung lazily to and fro in places where the cruising yachts and sea gypsies gathered to rest. Our horizon changed sometimes daily, friends made anew in every port, I was always on the look-out as we sashayed up under sail, for the tell-tale signs of other children, lifejackets slung over the boom, or kids' costumes drying in the shrouds, were a clear invitation to row over. In busier anchorages there was often an ever-changing group of boat kids, in other places there might be only one more vessel with children aboard, but we always saw each other every day and were best friends until we parted ways; age was unimportant, language not a barrier, there didn't seem such a thing as social class aboard the cruising boats, we all mixed and matched. I was free to roam, naked and barefoot, across desert islands, or snorkel over lively and vibrant coral reefs, through shadows of sharks without fear; we trekked rain-forested mountains and canoed crocodile crowded rivers. I stood my shortened watch on the helm while the others rested, the responsibility of keeping Jumbly Girl on course and the sails trimmed made me proud. I fished my own dinner, helped with all the chores aboard the boat, learnt to navigate and recognise the constellations, I knew the flags of all the countries we visited and the names of all the marine life we saw. I practised old seaman's sayings, such as 'one hand for yourself, one for the ship', and abided by them. We sang sea shanties in groups with other sailors, mother was a musician and her flutes or guitar strings would spring to life after a bottle of rum was opened, the drunken sailor would ripple out across the still waters of a protected anchorage, sung by strangers connected by ocean blood.

I was cleaved from this life mercilessly, from everything I had ever known, washed ashore on a foreign land where the toilet flushed with the press of a handle and rushed off all at once with a fierce growl, no jellyfish or phosphorescence floated in the bowl at night to make the toilet water sparkle and glow, I couldn't go and watch the fish enjoying the special treat after laboriously pumping the piston up and down 30 times. Opening the window to gaze up at stars left me bereft, all my stories gone, the constellations I loved to trace against the night sky as I recited their names and listened to the myths and legends surrounding them, replaced by the orange glow from street lamps that crept around the curtains of my window like alien fingers from which I hid. When they sold the boat, I was the Dong, left on land while the Jumblies sailed away, I felt as strange on land as though I had his wondrous, luminous nose upon my face. I tripped and stumbled over a surface that was too hard, too unyielding, no pitch or roll, rock or sway to compensate for. It was like hitting the bottom step wrong, with every footfall I made. Societies shoes aggravated my redundant sailors swagger, too tight for broad feet and splayed toes, to fit widthways they needed to be two sizes too big, so I was a clown, and school the circus in which I performed.

As a young adult I cast myself adrift from society, my home became an ancient Danish seine netter, destined for the breakers yard, I stepped aboard her and breathed in the musty smell of oakum, touched the tantalising remnants of the ocean that oozed from her planks as crystallised minerals. I slipped the heavy hemp lines that snubbed her bow as she tried to follow the running tide and hoisted her deep red sails so they fluttered in the breeze like the re-starting of her heart, I sheeted them in so we could point our bow towards the open ocean and unbroken horizon, to the company of dolphins and sea birds, salvation for us both. As I sailed, the deep wound life on land had slowly chafed into me, healed, painfully as salt rubbed into it, but salt is a great healer. My daughter's words, her desire, her wish to 'live on land', broke open that old scar, brought old memories to surface and painful times flooding back.

My children had grown up with the ocean's rocking lullaby below their heads, but from a young age they also had one foot firmly on solid ground, every morning I took them ashore in our little tender to climb the beach together and up the hill behind, they skipped in to school like all the other children, and I would run, barefoot and laughing, back down the hill to my boat, bobbing in the turquoise bay below me, resplendent in the morning sunshine. When I climbed onboard, I would wrap my arms around her stumpy main mast or lay my cheek against her warm deck. Designed to withstand the pressure of expanding ice if the sea froze around her while she fished, she is a work of art, salt laden oak planks over two inches thick, double oak frames each wider than the span of my outstretched hand, iron nails as long as my foot. She must float, like me, if you leave her too long on land her planks will dry out and shrink, cracks appearing everywhere, the fastenings that hold her together would become loose and eventually no amount of paying the devil would get her to float again. I understood her, my boat and her need to feel the ocean wave.

The children made friends at school, of course, they all lived in houses. They only wanted to be normal, accepted without undue judgement for a lifestyle choice that wasn't theirs. I dove deep, deep under the surface on which I am so comfortable, but this time it was a purposeful dive, I launched myself from the bulwarks, arms reaching up over my head to break the surface smoothly, creating not ripples or splashes, but roots and new growth. I ploughed into a fresh life standing tall and strong, reminding myself I was an adult and any choice I make is my own, regardless of who I make it for. With the money my lover bought me, her sixty tonnes of oak converted to 60,000 Euros cash in my pocket, I bought two acres of long abandoned agricultural land with an ancient stone building whose walls are a meter thick and stuffed with dry earth and lizards that scrabble around at night. A deep stone well plunges into cool, clear water that for six months I pulled up by hand, the feel of the rough rope against my skin was too familiar to swap for an electric pump and a tap to begin with, 'poc a poc' (little by little) is the slogan of the Balearic island where we live. The small house is surrounded by fruit and nut trees, cutting it off from the little lane that runs past the top field and shading it from the heat of a harsh summer sun. Deep in agricultural countryside it is as far from the ocean as I could get, afraid that the pull of the running tide would be too strong otherwise. Two kilometres away in the nearest village the children already know everyone in the small school, they flit between each other's houses like the sparrows between the branches of the swaying mulberry tree above me, I did not begrudge my daughters wish, sure in my heart that once they fly this nest I will return home. I did not want to be forced onto land again, the love for my children runs as deep as the deepest ocean current, I let my heart and mind eddy with love for them, releasing myself into life's counter current and letting myself swim with it, increasing the chances of success.

Now, finally, I am making peace with earth, creating empathy between my soul and land, open at last to a new experience of my own making. At dawn I wander dew dropped fields, always an early riser since long ago childhood days when a bucket of seawater would be sloshed across the poop deck by father, to slop over the rim of the hatch above my bunk, if I wasn't up and sitting at the saloon table by six AM sharp, ready to complete my daily schoolwork. In the early morning mist rises from the fields as from the ocean and the wind rustles the tree's leaves like a copy of rushing, tumbling waves. Instead of jigging for squid, or gathering algae and molluscs, I reach up to pluck fruit from the trees, or search the dark underbody of the hedgerows for the tender stalks of asparagus that shoot up unaided every spring. Each season brings a change to the land, from the lush waving green of winter and spring to the hard, cracked and rock-strewn desert of late summer, when it seems no life could survive in the baking earth. But the fruit trees thrive, little by little figs grow plump, then fat, bruising to a dark and squishy purple which splits easily open to reveal the sweetest, jammiest fruit I have ever tasted, I watch as nisperos transform from hard green buds into a yellowing fruit that deepens slowly to orange until one day all the fruit is ripe and ready. I eat them greedily, one after another, my children beside me, our chins running with their sharp sweetness.

Every fruit I try tastes better than anything I could imagine – the apples so crisp, so sweet, so juicy. The nuts so nutty. I am falling in love with the land in a way I hadn't thought possible. In late spring I watch, fascinated, as long, spindly, spine laden arms creep out of the ground, springing up from nothing into huge green caper bushes within weeks, suddenly they bloom, every bush studded with the most exquisite combination of three white petals that candy-coat the air in a sweet, rich musk, their long stamen wave elegantly from the flowers centre, a cerise pink rainbowing into violet at the bulbous tip, for months I live surrounded by a vast field of natural beauty that threatens to overload all but my sixth sense. I collect pails of unopened flower buds, soaking them in fresh water for three days and pickling enough to last me all year. It is a whole new lexicon for me to learn here, a new act to adapt to. I have learnt to keep chickens and caress the goat's udder to get the milk flowing, to pick the flower from the thistles growing almost as tall as me and make the milk curdle into cheese. I know how to gently waft smoke from smouldering pine needles at dutiful bees so I can carefully lift the capped honeycomb. I am making the most of my time on land, filling it with very earthly experiences. Because it is where I am now, watching my apples grow and ripen alongside the sweet oranges and bitter lemons.

But, my God, the Ocean, I miss it so much that when the wind blows, the palm fronds turn into the waves I love to hear, the waving grasses become the undulating swell I long to feel. I close my eyes and move, dancing in harmony to an ocean that is within me, coursing through my body in salty red rivers that ebb and flow like the tide. I am glad I have come to peace and made amends with the solid part of our world, but it doesn't stop me dreaming of the day I will be reunited with the only place I will ever call home.

STUNTED GROWTH

by Laura Goodfellow

There it is, right in front of me, erupting from a mulch of decaying leaves and rich coffee-coloured earth; a chaotic tangle of twisted branches spreading like the gnarled limbs of wizened hags from the belly-like trunk below. I wasn't sure if I'd still be able to find it, but the route my eight-year-old feet had first taken all those years ago lingered on the cusp of my memory and brought me back to this spot. To others, it must look like just another oak, there's nothing much to tell it apart from its neighbours, but this is our tree; I know what secrets lie hidden beneath the red, gold, and deep chestnut patchwork brown of its autumnal blanket.

Through a tear-stained curtain of memories, I can see us running there after school, you and me, past the chippy, scooting across the murky patch of wasteland and into the woods beyond. It's all changed; the chippy and the wasteland are gone, replaced by an exclusive housing development—two rows of bland, brown brick boxes with wooden blinds and shiny BMWs parked outside. The oak provided a backdrop to our childhood. A deep gash in the trunk led to a womb-like void, big enough for us to stand in. It was our den which we were prepared to defend with violence, if necessary when Barry and his gang tried to take it from us. We'd fly out howling like banshees brandishing sticks we had sharpened with my dad's Swiss army knife. Our hair wild with sticky weed, our faces smeared with mud. Running at them, we'd momentarily see the fear in their faces before Barry would say, 'Fucking weirdos, leave them.'

Relieved choruses of 'weirdos, weirdos' would follow before they all ran off laughing.

It was after one of Barry's failed coups that I first saw you cut yourself.

'We'll make a blood bond. He'll never get the den off us then; we'll be too strong. I've seen it done in film. We cut our hands then press them together so the blood touches, then we're friends forever.'

I remember how sick I felt as I watched the sticky red gash appear on your palm as you drew my dad's knife down it.

'Your turn.' You handed me the knife, expecting me to do the same, but I couldn't. I just couldn't bring myself to cut my hand. In the end, I picked a scab that produced a few drops of blood.

'Blood is blood.' You smiled as you pushed your palm against my knee.

Long summer days saw us swinging from dangerously frayed ropes slung over the only straight branch the old tree possessed. You were scared of heights, so it was my job to crawl across the branch, twenty-foot above the ground, to try and loop the rope around at least once while you stood below, assuring me you'd catch me if I fell. I remind my kids about the dangers of climbing trees now. I forget that once I did the same with you, with all the childhood abandon of unwavering faith in our own immortality.

We'd scour the undergrowth for discarded porn mags and giggle as the women's breasts were revealed to us as we flicked through the crumpled, damp pages. I used to wonder if you had the same tingling sensations in your trousers as I did. We tried shagging after one magazine-filled afternoon, just to see what it was like. Christ, we were like two fish floundering on dry land; awkward, embarrassing touches, fingers fumbling as we tried to undo each other's zips. We didn't have a bloody clue, but there again, what eleven-year-olds do? We ended up sitting outside the den, looking at the stars, sipping chemical-filled cider from a plastic bottle, and smoking roll-ups.

At thirteen, we shared our first joints in that den. We laughed so hard our cheeks ached as the tears streamed down our faces. What made us laugh, I can't remember, but in our weed-induced hysterics, it probably wasn't much.

It turned out you liked weed. You said it helped block out the voices in your head. The ones that held you prisoner, with their dark, deathly demands and made you so unpredictable. Never mind a dark cloud descending; it was like the whole fucking storm had come and sat on your shoulders. One misinterpreted word, and you would fly up swearing as your hands pressed so hard against your ears you almost looked as though you could have squashed your skull with all the ease of squeezing a strawberry.

Often, I'd find you sat alone in the den, quickly trying to conceal the knife in your hand and the wounds on your arms. I could see the pain in your eyes, I'd try to reach out, but you'd turn away. I never asked if you were ashamed that I'd caught you or angry that I'd interrupted.? I didn't really understand what was happening in your head, but I knew I hated those voices and their control over you.

We spent more and more time sitting in silence, me watching you retreating further and further away from those around you. I'd beg you to talk to me, but you'd shrug, shake your head and go back to whittling a piece of fallen branch. Slivers of wood curled around you like fallen leaves as your fingers worked deftly, carving soft curves and lines till you would throw a badger, fox, or a delicate spoon over to me. I found it hard to comprehend that those hands that had just created such beauty were the same hands that carved deep jagged lines into your arms.

Being in the den with you gave me the peace and quiet away from my five younger siblings that I yearned for. I'd sit and read while you whittled away. I wasn't a very sociable teenager; I was tall and gangly, and my regular clothing of ripped jeans and a black t-shirt, along with a musical taste that I inherited from my seventies rock-loving parents, marked me as different from the norm. I was cast to the outer rings of teenage society along with all the other misfits and weirdos not included but thankfully, not bullied either.

   Learning came easily to me, but for you, each word on the page was a struggle to read.

'I've got dyslexia.' You told me when you'd been assessed by a woman in a blue suit who had come into school especially to see you. 'I'm gonna get some help with my reading and writing.'

The extra support didn't help you. You were constantly in trouble. The other kids knew what buttons to press to make you react, and react you did, lashing out with your fists as groups of boys and girls goaded you on.

By the time you were fifteen, you had been expelled. The school didn't know how to help you any more than me or your exasperated family, countless psychiatrists, psychologists, or other doctors you saw, did. Each one would refer you to someone else or hand your mother a prescription for some drug or another that would help.

Sometimes you would improve for a few weeks, maybe even a couple of months, but then you would drift back to the dark places of your mind. Not even a light from the brightest of lighthouses would have reached you. I prayed for you, not to God; I didn't and still don't believe in him, but at night I cried out to anyone that could hear me. I felt you were being stolen from me by an unseen kidnapper that lurked in the dark places of your mind. I sat and watched as your world got smaller and smaller.

*

When I was offered a place at university two hundred miles away to study English Literature, I sat with you for days by our oak, under a makeshift shelter as a dry July gave way to torrential August rain, unable to find the words to tell you I was leaving. When I summoned up the courage to tell you, you turned away from me. I saw your shoulders shake as you told me you were proud of me and how I should go and never look back.

I did look back and look in as often as I could. To begin with, once every couple of weeks, I would turn up at the den, and you'd be there, blowing out a thick cloud of grey-green smoke from the joint in your hand.

I'd wince as I saw the new flashes of red crisscrossing your arm, angry and weeping as the scabs began to form when you offered me a drag. I'd always shake my head, but that never stopped you from offering.

'More for me.' You'd laugh before asking me about my life. I'd try and ask about you, how you were getting on, but you'd just shrug and flick your hand as though you were flicking something dirty and contagious from your fingers and press on with questioning me about my latest assignment or what book I was reading.

I returned home one weekend during my second year at uni, and you weren't at the den. I sent you a text and called, but you didn't reply. I went to your Mum's, but she hadn't seen you either, she thought you had come to meet me. Panic coursed through my body. Where were you? I walked the streets, searching for you, reaching your answerphone, time after time, until finally, I heard your voice at the other end.

'I've got a job,' you squealed in delight, 'I'm sorry I didn't meet you; I didn't want to tell anyone I was going for the interview in case I failed.'

'Asshole, you've had us all worried. Meet you at the den, and you can tell me all about it. And ring your Mum.'

Twenty minutes later, you were telling me all about your new job at the local animal shelter. You were going to help walk the dogs and muck out the horses. There was a light in your eyes, the first flicker of hope I had seen for a long time.

'New tablets and a better shrink. And I've given up the weed, got myself a counsellor to help me stay off it too.'

When I returned after my exams, you were waiting for me in the den. Your new job hadn't lasted; you'd lost your temper with another staff member and broken a window in anger. Luckily, they had agreed not to press charges on the condition you stayed away and paid for the damages. The light had gone out again. The acrid smell of weed lingered in the air, and you refused to talk. I left that day crying. I can't tell you if those tears were for you, me, or a friendship that seemed lost.

It seems cliched to say I'll never forget the day when two years after I'd left the den crying, your mother called me to say you'd taken your own life, but I won't. It is etched into my mind with all the permanency of an anchor tattooed on a sailor's arm. When the spectre of depression and voices that had kept you shackled so closely to it for most of your life had finally become too intense, too painful for you to carry on living with, you hung yourself from our tree.

Our tree? That made me fucking angry with you to begin with. I felt as though you had besmirched the sanctity of our childhood by choosing there to do it. Over time, I realised that there, at the oak, was where you had felt safe – felt free. It was the only place you could have done it. Mostly, I felt guilt for walking away that day and not telling you the truth. I'd made excuses texting you to say I wouldn't be home when I was. I couldn't face seeing you, you see. I was twenty; my uni life was entirely different from my life at school. I had friends. I went to parties. I joined the university writer's group and helped publish the university's magazine. I was no longer cast to the outer echelons of society, and I liked it. Days rolled into weeks and months; I barely messaged you, and when I did, you took longer and longer to reply to my texts until they petered out. I thought you were angry at me. You weren't, though, your ship was sinking, and you weren't trying to bail out.
Barry was at your funeral. He flicked back a rogue tendril of his Brylcreemed hair as he turned his tear-stained face towards me and nodded—a silent acknowledgment of the loss of a piece of our childhood jigsaw. We stood together near the back, cringing as we listened to the vicar delivering your soul to God. We bellowed out All Things Bright and Beautiful, your mother's choice. We clung to each other as the heavy red velvet curtain shrouded your coffin, and you descended into the fires below.

And now, here I am, thirty years later, back at this place of ghosts and dreams. The branch I nonchalantly tossed a rope over, the same one you purposefully tied a rope to, has gone. Cut down. A dark circular scar is the only evidence of its existence. My fingers tingle and quiver as I stretch my hand out; I want to touch it, to touch you, but it's too high.

The bark is rough beneath my hands as I reach around the trunk, trying to encircle it with my arms, pressing myself hard against it, trying to reach into its very heart and find you. Are you playing in the trees now or hiding in the den? Perhaps you are part of the tree now? I can't help but cry; the sense of you, of your essence, lingers all around this place and overwhelms me. Tears of years of guilt, regret, and anger spill out all at once as I sink to my knees.

Time has drifted, and darkness is beginning to creep into the woods. Shadows dart amongst the trees, and I can't help but wonder if they are the same shadows that took you from me. There were days when I wanted to follow you to escape the guilt and sadness that I felt. I thought that maybe if I found you, I could bring you back. My life juddered to a halt. I was held in the past, stuck like a fly twitching on a spider's web as my life slowly ebbed away.

Is that you wrapping around me in the wind, making the canopy rustle and the leaves dance in the spiralling air? As stillness returns and they float silently back to earth, a feeling of peace is growing within me.

The time has come for me to leave; two teenage boys are waiting patiently with Barry in the car. Yes, Barry, our nemesis. We kept in touch after your funeral. He understood my pain and was there for me in a way; I am so sorry I wasn't for you. He brought a bucket and helped me bail, and we fell in love.

I won't return here, at least not yet anyway. When I do, it will be to step through into the womb of our oak and sit in our den with you, but until that day, goodbye, my dearest friend, my first love. Be the wind in the leaves, the sweet summer rain, and the first snow of winter, be the heart of the oak, be at peace, my fellow warrior.

THE KEENING

by C. S. Parks

Captain Erasmus Arlington pulled up the collar of his dark navy pea coat as the cold, biting wind whistled across the bow of the ship. It was a vain attempt to keep its gnashing teeth from reaching bare skin. The Captain scanned the darkness beyond, grateful for every cresting wave that caught the moonlight, giving him some orientation in the gloom as the Pride of Beulah's sleek hull pushed slowly through the sea.

'Forty-Three Fathoms,' yelled a voice from the starboard side of the ship.

'4 knots,' a rough, lowland voice from the stern replied.

'Twenty-two degrees, ahead clear.' The raspy voice of a man called McTavish called from high above in the crow's nest.

The Captain relaxed slightly and allowed his mind to wander for a moment.

He lay still, not daring to move lest he disturbed the vision wrapped in his arms. The early morning sun was streaming through the slatted window, catching on the wisps of her flaxen hair, reminding him of the sundogs that he had seen while sailing the cold north. He held the image in his mind, letting it wash over him. A perfect moment.

A warning of an incoming fog from the lookout above focused the Captain's mind. On their current bearing, the ship should be able to avoid the thickest part of the haar. Its thinner parts reached out like tendrils, trying to entwine themselves like ivy around the Pride's mast. Thankfully, they were just out of reach. The thick, lactescent centre seemed to suck all the joy out of the world. The Captain's heart sank just thinking about being lost in such a fog and sailing so close to the mainland; they would be unable to see the craggy rock formations that littered the shallows. The status report echoed once more around the ship, reassuring him all was well.

As he walked back from collecting the cordwood from the small lean-to shack nearby. He could hear the sounds of splashing water and singing. Her voice entranced him. He stood outside the door for a moment letting the melancholic melody enthral him, feeling a pull, drawing him closer. Finally, he slowly opened the door and entered. He had a dreamy, lopsided smile on his face. Maya lay in the tin bath, eyes closed and the milky water concealing her nakedness. She was lost in rapture. Her song of sweet sadness filled the Captain's cabin. His heart felt light and joyous. He came up behind her and lightly kissed the side of her neck. She smiled, pulling him closer to her. Their lips touched. A perfect moment.

'Helm! Adjust ye bearing to thirty degrees,' The rasping Scottish voice of McTavish bellowed from the crow's nest. 'Quick man! Or we are all doomed!'

The Pride pitched aggressively, as the man known only as "Dora's boy" on the helm, hand over hand turned the ship's wheel with force. No one knew his actual name and in truth, he seemed to have forgotten it over time. He was brought on to the ship as a favour to an old friend of the crew and simply introduced as "Dora's boy". The name stuck.

The Captain appraised the new bearing for a moment, with a growing realisation that this course was taking the Pride into the centre of the brume.

'Crow's! Why have we changed bearing?' he yelled.

'Canny ya not hear it Cap'ain,' came the reply.

He turned his head, straining his ears. He could hear nothing but the crashing of waves as the bow broke water and the rush of wind as it whipped around the rigging. The thick fog started to encompass the ship, seemingly reducing the ship to a slow ahead speed. The sails above started to flap wildly as they desperately tried to regain their grasp on the wind. A woeful vexing inside his head started to gnaw away at him. He felt a keen urgency, a tightening in his chest as if a murderous constrictor had coiled around him, giving rise to panic.

'Crow's! Explain this bearing!'

The was a pause. It felt like a lifetime to the Captain.

'Oh Cap'ain, it be the most beautiful song I ever heard in me life. Sweeter than the songs me mama use to sing to me as a bairn.'

The Captain looked skyward, allowing his eyes to focus for a moment, disbelieving his own eyes. The large main sail below the crow's nest was flapping furiously as if it were frantically trying to draw attention to the unfolding drama. McTavish had climbed out of the crow's nest. Like a tightrope walker, his arms were stretched out straight, walking the line between life and death on the boom. One sudden pitch or roll of the Pride would send him to his death, however, he seemed to anticipate every movement the undulating sea could offer.

'Get down this instant you fool!'

The Captain's order was caught up in the wind and swirled away, lost within the cries of the rest of the crew. McTavish had now reached the end of the boom. The wind caught his wild, auburn hair, swirling it all around his face, catching in his wiry beard, obscuring his features. His arms opened wider like a man seeking absolution for his sins. He pitched forward. His body remained cruciform as he plummeted. His head struck the taffrail of the Pride with a sickening thud that every man on board felt in their very soul. A fine red mist filled the area for the briefest moment and then was lost in the wind and sea spray. The world slipped away from the Captain as the Pride held her collective breath, shocked.

There seemed a sadness in Maya today. Her usual lightness had wilted into nervousness. The fabric on the cuff of her dress had become frayed by the constant pulling on a loose thread. She laid with her head on his lap. He was gently running his hand over her temple and feeling the softness of her hair in his fingertips.

'What's wrong my love?' he said with a softness in his voice, barely audible, not daring, in truth to ruin this perfect moment.

She turned to him; her eyes full of sorrow, a single tear weaving a trail down her cheek.

The Pride lurched violently to a full stop, every joint of her oak hull protested, making its feelings known with a series of shuddering cracks. The Captain wrapped his fingers around one of the guide ropes as the Pride pitched to one side, his knuckles turning white with the exertion. His boots failing to find purchase on the sodden deck slipped and he landed heavily, exploding the air out of his lungs. Through the fog, he could hear the wails from the rest of the crew. Voices calling out in terror from all around him; he tried to make sense through his own daze.

'Rocks, we've hit rocks!' an unknown voice said, panicked and shrill.

The Captain tried to push himself up, his eyes felt unfocused, and he had a nauseous feeling rising from within him. He touched his head and felt a sticky warmth. He must have stuck his head as he fell, he thought. He pulled himself to his feet noting that the Pride was now resting at an oblique angle. To his right, through the fog, he could see the vague outline of one of the crew that he recognised as Dora's Boy. He was slumped in a seated position, holding his head and groaning. The Captain attempted a step towards him, but his head swirled once more, and the bile in his stomach forced its way out of him with a loud retching sound, burning his throat. He sank back down to his haunches and tried to refocus. As he wiped the tears stinging his eyes, a shadow passed between the two men. The fog swirled filling the space it left, leaving a miasma in its wake.

There was a heavy silence hanging in the cabin. The Captain could not comprehend the words Maya had spoken. He was an experienced sailor, well versed in the fairy tales that the older sailors told the young'uns to keep them a wake at night, but this, this was different. Maya stood in front of him, her arms loose by her side, her head tilted downwards but her eyes still looked deep into him. He shook his head and walked out of the door. He could hear Maya sobbing, as he walked across the sun-bleached grass towards the beach. The sun was just starting to set behind the cabin with shades of burnt orange, hot pinks, reds and molten yellows. To the Captain, it looked as if his whole world was on fire. Nothing was going to be perfect ever again.

'Your voice, that song. I have never heard such sweet songs of love,' said Dora's Boy 'Let me hold you my lov-.'

The rest of the words were cut short, replaced with a breathless gurgling sound, reminding the Captain of the sound the bilge pump makes when it is blocked. This sound was quickly replaced by the sound of a fierce argument just to the left of the Captain.

'She is mine!' yelled one man.

'Never! She sings her songs for me alone!' said another his voice full of anger.

The first man struck the second with his knife. It sliced easily through the flesh of his throat and for a second his eyes flashed anger, and then all life vanished. His carcass thumped to the floor like a discarded piece of meat. The executioner turned towards the Captain; his eyes wild with desperation.

'I know you want her! She is mine! She sings for me!'

He lunged at the Captain, who shifted his body to the side to avoid the blow, however, he was too slow, the knife dug deep into his left shoulder, hitting bone. Pain surged through his body and as a reflex he kicked out with the heel of his boot. He caught his assailant powerfully in the midriff, staggering him backwards a few paces. The Captain pulled the knife from his shoulder and prepared for the next attack. He faced the man, whose rotten teeth were visible behind a wild sneer. His second lunge was halted abruptly. Long talons slowly closed around his neck, drawing blood as they met his skin. Unable to turn his head his eyes wildly darted from side to side. The Captain realised the man's feet were no longer on the deck. The more he gasped for air the tighter the grip seemed to become, the sound of bones cracking punctuating the air. His eyes started to bulge, and the vessels became engorged with blood. There was a soft popping sound and sanguine tears fell onto his cheeks. His mouth gaped in a silent scream as his chest exploded, spraying blood across the deck; his still-beating heart in the grip of another set of bloodied talons. His body was then ripped in two and discarded.

The Captain used the cuff of his coat to wipe the blood from his face. Through the mist, the shadow moved towards him. Its atrocious eyes luminant green, unblinking on its approach. There was no song for the Captain. The gnawing sensation he felt before became a dejected wailing, deep within him.

A howl echoed off the rock faces surrounding the cove. The Captain ran as fast as he could in the direction of the sound. There he found Maya on the sand, dragging herself towards the sea. Her skin was cracked and bloody. Her hair falling out in clumps. The Captain lifted her in his arms, and she whispered in his ear. He nodded and carried her into the waves up to his chest. As the waves hit her body, she began thrashing in his arms. He let her go. His perfect Maya vanished into the waves.

The siren stood before the Captain. Her skin was covered in pearlescent scales, her limbs long and rangy.
'My love?' said the Captain. A tear rolled down his cheek.
The siren tilted her head to one side and the Captain was sure he saw a flicker of recognition flash across her face. In an instant, she was on him. Her breath smelt like death, rancid and abhorrent. Her rank tongue slowly licked the tear off his cheek and then she

kissed him.

The Captain felt his lung tighten as they filled with the salty seawater. He tried to take a breath; unable he felt a panic spread across him. He looked deep into her eyes. He raised the knife in his hand. It felt cold and hard, the blade caught a glint off the moon. He placed the knife over her chest. He felt resistance at first, but then the keen blade sliced through her flesh and into her heart. A cold sticky fluid spilt over his hands and the two bodies dropped to the deck, entwined like a lover's embrace. He held her tight to him and kissed her head. As his lungs filled with icy water, his life slipped away; he had his last thought.

A perfect moment.

CLEARING UP
THE MESS

by Peter Long

In 2006 I found a therapist that I finally clicked with. This coincided with finding the correct anti-depression medication, or at least a cocktail that put me on a more even keel so that I could listen to myself and my therapist without black dog barking so loud to drown out any rationale.

With my new found clear head, I could think about the man I wanted to be and make steps towards becoming that man. But not all of us get to write our own personalities. Sometimes we are forced into a mould. Thankfully I have never been in any of the armed forces because war is a time in which people are often moulded against their will.

The story I am telling is an amalgamation of stories I have been told by family members. One is in World War II when, as a boy, my Uncle witnessed both houses either side of his being hit by bombs; and the second is where my Grandfather had a grenade thrown into his tank and emerged the only survivor. The story is not a diarised account of what happened to these people, although I am convinced those stories would indeed be worth reading, rather it is concerned with the shape of the mould; how they accepted or fought against it and if they broke free, as I long to break free of the depression that overwhelms me.

The following account is centred around Mansueto Delucca, the son of a rich businessman in the Tuscan region of Italy. The family fortune was from the production of olive oil and a town had sprung up around their extensive olive groves, with most people working in the factories or lush groves. The father, who birthed the company, was a man of principle and treated the town's people well. Mansueto however, was a son who, despite his father's teachings, simply wanted to sit back on his allowance and live the romantic life of the poet. Except without the hard work it takes to hone the wit and insight of a poet. If he had been born in this century he would surely be on a reality TV show. His father's greatness, his honest and fair approach to business and life had rubbed off on Mansueto, but it took an extreme act for the son to realise his father's wisdom.

Mansueto's father died a peaceful death just before World War II was declared. His two sisters desired to run the company which meant Mansueto could live his romantic life, as long as his allowance was not interrupted. His sisters moved away from the rural family home and headed for the hustle and bustle of Milan, where they were visited by Mansueto who freely admitted in letters that he wished to 'sow his oats and punish his liver'!

The invasion of Austria and Poland meant nothing to him. When war was declared and Mussolini sent troops to slow Hitler down, Mansueto's only concern was whether the party scene would be closed down or not. He didn't even notice the headlines reporting of Mussolini "changing sides" and aligning with the Nazis. He was attending a private party in a museum in the centre of Milan the very next night. To him, and a lot of Italians, especially the elite, the war was a far off trifle, dealt with by those that deal with that sort of thing. If Italy's National Fascist Party, the PNF, were ever going to succeed at anything in the formal ball of politics, then war should be placed highly on their dance card.

These private parties were attended by the bourgeois elite; principally young men spending money and young women chasing money. They would start loud, the dance floor packed, the expensive tipples flowing like water, before the lights turned low, the music softened and the crowd retreated to the booths for night time debauchery. Mansueto was that night, as usual, in one of the best booths, joined by his friend and heir to a fashion house, Allesandro, and four buxom girls. Allesandro set up absinthe cocktails, fancying himself a follower of Baudelaire's footsteps. Mansueto laced each sugar cube with a drop of laudanum before pouring the absinthe over and into the glass.

'To the pursuit of hedonism!' toasted Alessandro.

'Alla nostra salute!' replied Mansueto and they both drained their glasses of the potent aniseed cocktail.

As they knocked their empty glasses on the table the building shook once. Then again as they stared at each other open mouthed, the shaking accompanied by a low booming noise that could wake the dead. Following the throng to the exit, Mansueto expected to emerge into darkness, but that part came later. The fires lit up the night brighter than the day and the group followed the dispersing crowd of gentlemen buttoning up their trousers and women wearing nothing but heels and pearls into the centre of the piazza. All around them was destruction, a bus had disappeared into a hole in the road, rubble, dust, metal and fire surrounded them and as Mansueto span around the last thing he would remember from that night was seeing a wave of rubble and fire either side of the unscarred building from which he had just emerged. They had missed being killed by inches. It was all too much for the pampered man-child and he fainted.

Once home, Mansueto emerged into his own darkness. Isolating himself he imbibed anything alcoholic. Longing not to feel at all, he saw a black eternity spreading out endlessly in front of him. A constant night under a freezing moon. His mind raced towards something to hold on to, but his life had been shallow and he found no anchor to tie on to; like running in a murky forest towards nothingness. He did this again and again, over and over until he heard his Father's voice with atoms of fatherly advice that slowly became amoebas, eventually rising up in his mind until they became sentient beings of their own. He began to look around him, read the newspapers and listen to the wireless. Mussolini had made a mess of the once proud nation of Italy and the Germans were coming. He was a man with the means to do something. He had to do something; and he had to do it now.

The blackness that Mansueto felt is an amalgamation of my own feelings and descriptions from my Uncle and Grandfather. The latter returned from war and fell into depression, whereas my Uncle was too young to understand the lasting effect of seeing how close he had come to death in the night. It did serve as an image that made him feel that he had to do something great with his life because 'you never know when your number is up'. He went on to be a Director of a major department store and once he even met the Queen. However, family happiness eluded him until much later in life. He retired early due to 'health issues', which he later confided in me had been a long and clinging depression. He told me once that in his therapy, a lot of issues he had led him back to the image of his unscathed house amongst the destruction of the houses either side.

There was practically no post war mental health help and my Grandfather lived with his experience pushed down to the basement of his mind. After initially being very withdrawn, he managed, by sheer force of willpower, to join in with the rebuilding of Britain and provide for his family in post war times. I don't know if he ever really recovered. This is a story that many who serve in the armed forces share, and a story that must be concluded with "... and I'm glad we don't do it that way anymore."

I have no story of heroism to tell. I have not been the only survivor of anything and have never had a particularly close shave with death, and this only serves to make the personal justification of depression worse. A common mantra of the depressed and those around them is that 'there's nothing wrong with you, pull yourself together'. There are some days when I do have to pull myself up, puff my chest out and stiffen my upper lip just to get going, as I imagine my Grandfather did. Once I am going however, I am usually on a roll and can actually achieve a lot in a day. Mostly real things. I feed my family. I keep my children safe. I interact with them and provide a positive influence, education, etiquette and decency. These are the things my Uncle wished he could have done with his children rather than spending so much of his life chasing money, as he said many times until his death in 2019.

And so my daily mantra is; if these are the only things I do in a day, then surely that day has not been wasted.

Rest easy those who have given themselves over to our freedom. May we not squander that freedom and understand what life is truly about, and have that understanding endure infinitely, interminably and unequivocally.

SOLO

by Mandy Kerr

Mum,

I know that you are worried about me going away on my own to a far-flung country, and that you are concerned about the political unrest in the 'Far East' as you put it (despite being relatively clueless about the political unrest here in England), but I will message you every day to reassure you. I have thus far reached the age of 55, bought a house, held down a job and managed to not kill my children. I will be fine.

Gatwick.

I remain unradicalised. The ISIS recruitment stand was unmanned; I think he was at lunch. Not been swept off my feet yet by a Turkish fisherman with a large gulet, but they are few and far between around the airport. My flight has been called, so see you on the other side. (No, not the spiritual other side..) Please don't worry about me.

Day One.

I have avoided militant Syrian insurgents so far. I thought I saw one at Dalaman airport, but it turned out to be a grumpy Costa Coffee employee having a quick ciggy on his break. Lovely apartment in the town where Icarus fell to earth after his wings tragically melted. Well, not actually in the town centre, in the sea. I feel this must mean something but haven't worked out what it is yet. Discovered, to my horror, that you can take a Kindle to Turkey but can't bring it back again. What sort of weird regulation is that?

Surely there must be some kind of Kindle mountain there by now? I have survived day one.

Day Two.
This morning I made two new feline friends. (Anya, and an unnamed male with huge cat balls). I discovered that Turkish cats shout a lot and eat entire bags of crisps while blatantly staring you in the eye. I had to chase them round the balcony to retrieve my cheese and onion Lays (when in Rome…). I might head into the mountains shortly to search for bears, mountain lions and an alleged Daesh training camp. (Joking Mother). Rest assured I am still alive.

Day Three.
Saw a wild tortoise. Was hoping for a mountain lion really but beggars can't be choosers. Discovered that Anya the cat is actually Tanya the cat, which explains why she was ignoring me. And the unnamed cat is, in fact, called George, a name I feel doesn't do justice to his majestic masculinity. Dithered about going out in a strapless dress, but couldn't work out whether that was out of respect for the Muslim culture or a compulsion to keep my bingo wings under cover. I went for it anyway but kept my fingers crossed that I wouldn't be stoned to death as a Western strumpet. I have a feeling that sadly my strumpet days are well behind me so it should be fine.
Still, I got to meet and be attacked by another cat (just a flesh wound and yes, my tetanus shots are up to date), and even saw a display of some cool skulls arranged on a fence. I think this might have been Ed Gein's house, but I declined to go in for the obligatory Turkish tea. The phrase 'I've had a skinful' may have been misinterpreted. Against the odds I'm still alive.

Day Four.
Another wing meltingly hot day. Even my eyeliner pencil has become impotent, and my iPhone informed me that it was going on strike due to unacceptable working conditions. My task for

today, to find a boat trip. When I got to the harbour I was faced with a Libran nightmare. Dozens of boats all promising to be the Best. Boat. Trip. Ever. Even I know that this cannot be possible. What if I happen to choose the boat skippered by a disillusioned captain who has picked today to be the day that he takes his final voyage and goes down with his ship? I can't risk that. To avoid terrorism but fall prey to a bitter seaman with suicidal tendencies and possible mother issues? I decided to take a few names and do some research ready for tomorrow. Luckily, as I wandered back, I bumped into local restauranteur Ramazan, whose best friend Ahmet is a captain wouldn't you know.

'Say Ramazan sent you and Ahmet will make sure that you are looked after very well.' As he spoke, he winked in what I presume he intended as a gesture of reassurance, but I have seen a few films along these lines, and they generally don't end well to say the least. Sali at the restaurant next door promised me fresh squid and octopus when the fishing boat comes in at four. He offered me a romantic table on the water and looked genuinely distraught at my plight when I requested a romantic table for one. He told me I was a very beautiful lady which, considering I was covered in sweat with fingers like sausages and wild humidity frizzed hair (remember Monica in that episode of Friends?), I took with a pinch of salt. Although I think I saw a genuine tear of pity and compassion in his eye. Wandering back for a swim, the incessant chirp of insects meant I was unable to get the opening bars of Club Tropicana out of my head...

I haven't spoken to one single English person here. No Dave and Sue from Southampton or Wendy and Mike from Manchester. Just the locals who make my breakfast, clean my room, bring my vodka, and serve my dinner. They are all charming, helpful, speak very little English, but are happy to try to have a chat nevertheless, and love it when I try to say hello, please and thank you in Turkish. That's what being abroad should be all about surely? Needless to say, I remain alive and well.

Day Five.

Us Scots are definitely not genetically designed for such temperatures. As Woody Allen once said, 'I don't tan, I stroke.' Lazing by the pool for the day has given me the opportunity to watch the ebb and flow of guests at the apartments. The benevolent group of ladies of a certain age who were obviously here on some kind of yoga retreat (the proliferation of mandala tattoos and fringed kimonos gave it away), leaving parting gifts of cherries and strawberries for the two lovely maids who work all day with smiles, humour and literally no idea what you are saying to them. Also, excitingly, the arrival of the first English voice I've heard so far. He is called John, is from up north (Burnley, Bolton, Barnsley?), has a very loud voice, and appeared to be drunk on arrival. Or maybe not, it's hard to tell with some people. Anyway, he hung out at reception with the ever patient, ever present manager, who was trying to explain to him the English meanings for Trump and wanker. (hand gestures included). This was punctuated by John's regular cries of 'Chop chop!' to the friendly maids who, I must say, took it all in very good spirit. He then flung himself into the pool and started to sing Especially for you at the manager who, by this point, was looking slightly baffled. As was I by this time, and I slunk down behind my book and sunglasses in case John decided to include me in his duet for one. Thankfully, he didn't. I have survived another day.

Day Six.
Ok, so you know I said it was hot before? That was literally just the warmup. I don't think there's even a word for this. It would be more of a strangled gasp which I'm not sure how to spell. As I was walking out, Olgun, the owner here, stared incredulously at me and gasped,
   'Hat?? Hat!!'
I told him I didn't have one, but wrapped a gauzy black scarf over my head, which I'm pretty sure would just magnify the direct heat on my brain. However, he seemed placated, even approving, as he told me that now I looked like a Muslim. Maybe this is how radicalisation starts? By forgetting a hat.

Anyway, the reason I'm still not on a boat is that I had such a bad night's sleep, alternating between turning the air con on (too noisy) and off (too hot), that I turned my alarm off and didn't wake up until 10 am. I'm buying and eating stuff without having a clue what it is, taking a wild guess that peyniri is much more likely to be cheese than mountain lion penis.

I went to the Marina with two boats in mind. How do I choose between them? Does one captain look more trustworthy than the other? One more unhinged? Do I choose by a glint/twitch of the eye or do I hand out a psychometric questionnaire? (I feel valued in my job: strongly agree, agree, neutral, disagree, strongly disagree). I went by gut instinct and jumped on the Aviva 2. The other boat had already buggered off anyway.

So I headed out to sea feeling like a cross between Marco Polo and Simon le Bon in the Rio video...

There have been many captains in history; Captain Ahab, Captain Birdseye, Captain Pugwash, Captain and Tennille (one for the over 50s, keeping it current), and now Captain Ahmet. Amazing day, great food, and lots of stops for swimming (desperately trying not to think of Deep Blue Sea, Jaws, or indeed any film with sharks or other aquatic killers). Luckily, I'm not one of these people who need to be able to feel the floor under my feet; fathoms of deep green sea beneath, warm ocean all around, Cleopatra's stomping ground and a true taste of Turkey. It's only the Muezzin calling the faithful to prayer at 4.30am that makes me think sod this, I'm too lazy to be Muslim. Day six successfully survived.

Day Seven.

Well, I'd hoped to do my final update in Turkey, but my cheap iPhone charger had other ideas and packed up (damn you Poundland!). Maybe it was finally sick of all the photos of yachts. Consequently, and perhaps fittingly, it's last gasp was a message from Captain Ahmet last night. Enigmatically it read 'Good Evening'. I guess I'll never know what it meant (possibly good evening?) How he even got my number remains a mystery, but I blame some Turkish ladies I met on the boat. It's a shame I didn't get a picture to show you, as he wasn't your stereotypical captain. He had a man bun and said he liked going to 'disco clubs'. Instead of his photo, I'm taking one which shows the flagrant disregard for health and safety found in Turkish bathrooms (you can't take a kindle out of the country, but you can have a live electrical socket in the shower apparently). Also, a sneaky one of Northern John. I felt a bit like David Attenborough taking that one. I'd thought having a late flight today would be a bonus, but in reality, you're up, packed, turfed out of your air-conditioned cocoon, and left in a sweaty limbo. I got a nice hug from the cleaning lady, and Olgun's son (confusingly also called Ramazan) wants you to visit. Five hours wait for transport, then three hours wait at the airport, where I shared a brilliantly British, outraged conversation about the price of a cup of tea. I have maintained a ten to one water to vodka ratio, learned how to suck out a fish brain and read six novels. More importantly, no one died. Looking forward to seeing you soon.

P.S. can you recommend a good self-tan? I went away the colour of milk and have returned the colour of milk just on the turn. Woody was spot on.

SIR GAWAIN AND THE GREEN KNIGHT REIMAGINED.

Amazement seized their minds,
no soul had ever seen
a knight of such a kind –
entirely emerald green.

(SIR GAWAIN AND THE GREEN KNIGHT – SIMON ARMITAGE)

Some of us studied Simon Armitage's translation of his ancient poem and inspired by his words we present to you, in part or full, our reimaginings of this great tale.

THE KNIGHT, THE GIANT AND THE LADY

by Mandy Kerr

There was once a Lord and Lady who lived in a great castle in the middle of a forest. The Lady was known as the most beautiful in the land, with eyes as green as emeralds and hair as dark as a raven's wing. She had, however, entered into marriage to please her father and not for any true feeling towards her husband. She loved her father dearly, and willingly accepted her betrothal, which was created to unite two great families. Her husband, Lord Bertilak, spent his days hunting the stags and the boars of the forest, but did not treat her unkindly so she was tolerably happy.

Every year, on All Hallows Evening, a giant who lived in the woods, came into the nearby village and stole a newborn child, tore it from the breast of its distraught mother, and rode off with it on his mighty steed. The villagers said that the giant was as tall as the gibbet which stood at the crossroads and formed as if of nature herself. For his limbs were like the boughs of a great oak tree and his hair was a mass of wild ivy. This upset the Lady greatly, as although she had not been blessed with children herself, she was as kind as she was beautiful, and it distressed her to see faithful servants in such pain. She decided to summon a knight to rid the village of this evil giant and so sent a message to Camelot and requested the service of its bravest knight in exchange for as much gold as he could carry home.

After the moon had completed one full cycle, there appeared a figure astride a dark mount who knocked loudly on the castle gate. A servant answered his knock and knew at once that this was a man of courtly bearing, as he was clothed in the finest mail and fur, and his sword was as expertly crafted as Excalibur itself. He bade Gawain enter and led him to a chamber where the Lady sat.

'I am Sir Gawain from the court of King Arthur', said the knight, with a deep bow. The Lady made him welcome, for her husband was not at home, and told him of the giant which plagued them.

'I beg you to slay this foul demon who is blighting our land good sir', she said. 'My husband is a good man, but not a warrior, and more taken with the hunting of animals than of giants. Please avail yourself of our hospitality this night, for tomorrow is All Hallows, and I fear another babe will be lost.'

Sir Gawain, as befits a knight of great bravery and honour, accepted the challenge, and set off the next morning, his sword shining in the bright, morning sun. As he rode through the hamlet, villagers came out to see the brave knight for word had spread of his noble quest.

'God speed!', cried a woman. 'I lost my child to the devil five years past. May your journey be protected by the spirits of the wood. Follow yonder path until you come to a dark place where no birds sing, and there you will find your foe.' Gawain thanked the woman and set his steed in the direction of his fate.

Presently he came upon a large brown bear, its leg caught in the jaws of a bear trap. It twisted and turned, shaking its shaggy head in distress.

'Please help me good sir', cried the bear, 'and I will see your kindness is rewarded'. So, Gawain set the bear free of its iron prison and in return the bear handed him a small pouch of forest mushrooms.

'These will ensure that any injury which may befall you will be swiftly healed.' He growled and ran off into the trees. Gawain tucked the pouch into his belt and carried on his way through the dappled forest.

After awhile he came upon a russet fox, its bushy tail snarled up in a patch of prickly brambles. The poor creature was caught fast, and it snapped its jaws this way and that in an effort to free itself.

'Please help me good sir', barked the fox, 'and I will see your kindness is rewarded.' So, Gawain set about untangling the fox's brush from the thorny thicket, and in return the fox gave him a small bag of herbs.

'These will make you fleet of foot and swift of movement.' Said the fox and trotted away through the glade. Gawain tucked the bag into his belt and carried on through the woods. He rode awhile further until he chanced upon a stag whose antlers were intertwined among the gnarled branches of a mighty oak tree. It stamped its hooves and tossed its head to no avail.

'Please help me good sir', bayed the stag, 'and I will see your kindness is rewarded.' So, Gawain untwisted the creature's antlers from the boughs of the tree and in return the stag gave him a small vial of potion.

'Anoint your blade with this liquid and any wound you inflict shall prove mortal to your enemy.' He whinnied and galloped off into the forest. Gawain added the vial to a bag at his waist and pressed his heels to the flanks of his mount. The sun was low and getting ever lower as he continued on the rocky path which wound ever downwards towards the verdant home of the giant. The trees became ever thicker and darker as he went, and the noises of the forest quieted as if nature itself forsook this wicked place.

At last, he reached a woody throne on which sat a man seemingly created of boughs and leaves. Thorny vines encircled his head, and it was as if branches sprouted from his very beard. A mighty axe lay across his knee, gripped in a gnarly hand. Gawain dismounted and stood before the fearsome sight. He held aloft his glittering sword and his hand was steady and sure. The giant rose to the height of two men and raised his axe, holding Gawain in his gaze. Gawain was a knight of great cunning who had heeded the words of the forest creatures and had eaten the mushrooms and swallowed the herbs and tempered his sword with the magic elixir. So, the first blow from the giant's axe inflicted only a flesh wound which healed in an instant, and the second blow he dodged with ease. In return his sword grazed the giant's knee which was as thick and solid as a tree trunk, but the wound was fatal nonetheless and the giant crashed to the ground as if felled.

Gawain returned with haste to the castle and the Lady once more welcomed him in.

'Good Lady, I have slain your giant and all shall now be well. I have brought you his head in this velvet bag as proof of my honour and valour.'

'Good Sir Gawain, we are forever in your debt. The tales of your deeds were truly spoken, for you are in truth a man of great bravery. I will see that you are rewarded for your great service.'

Then Gawain emptied the bag onto the floor and the Lady cried out in shock, for they were the eyes of her husband which stared back at her.

'Good sir Gawain, what magic is this? My Lord and the giant are one and the same?'

'I cannot say what enchantment must have befallen your Lord, but where once evil walked, now there is none, so do not be sad, I pray.'

Gawain took pity on this tragic widow whose eyes were as green as the emerald forest, remained at the castle, and in the fullness of time the two were married. The village rejoiced, for the giant was dead and their new-borns were saved, and the Lady and her Knight lived happily ever after.

SIR GAWAIN AND THE GREEN KNIGHT

by Laura Goodfellow

Winter had come to King Arthur's court! Snow lay roundabout in soft fluffy mounds, that sparkled like giant meringues in the pink glow of evening sunlight. Inside the Castle, Lords and Ladies from all over the Kingdom had gathered to celebrate Christmastime with the King. For two whole weeks, a plethora of song, music and laughter had filled the air. The Lords and Ladies had danced together, the fabric of the Ladies' dresses swishing, as they spun and whirred around the hall in joyous rapture. Oh, how gay and bright were the scenes! Now the final night had come, the night of the New Year, when the biggest and most extravagant feast of the celebration would be served.

 None had enjoyed the celebrations more than the Knights of the Round Table, who were now drinking their fill of beer and wine from the pottery jugs placed on the table and laughing loudly as they recounted events from the day's tournament of jousting and swordplay. Suddenly, their laughter stopped and the whole room fell silent as the sound of a trumpet heralded the arrival of the King and his beautiful Queen, Guinevere. Each of the Knights stood up from their chairs and bowed their heads in quiet reverence as the King and Queen passed by on their way to take their seats on their thrones. As soon as they were seated, the Knights sat down again and everyone waited for the King to speak. Taking to his feet again, the King began,

'My dear Queen, Lords, Ladies and my loyal Knights, I bid you a warm welcome on this our last night together, a most auspicious of nights, that of the New Year.' Cheers and cries of 'Noel, Noel, Noel' greeted the King's words.

'Tonight, we will feast!' he continued 'We will supp the wine of friendship! We will dance until the sun dawns on the first day of the year!' More cries of 'Noel, Noel, Noel' came from the assembled throng.

'Let the feasting begin!' the King cried as the thumped his fist down on the table.

At the King's command, the sound of pipes and drums could be heard, as plates and bowls appeared from the kitchen, some were filled with steaming soup, some piled high with Pheasants, Partridges, and sweetmeats, some with bread and cheese. The final silver platter was carried in by four young men, all dressed in red and green. Upon the platter, laid a huge wild boar, its eyes dull and lifeless, its mouth open revealing fearsome tusks. Oh, what a feast it was! The King sat, observing, but not a crumb of bread nor a drop of wine did he eat.

'My Lord, why do you not eat?' enquired the Bishop who was sitting to the right of the Queen, 'Does the food not satisfy you?'

'Yes, yes, yes,' replied the King 'the feast will in time satisfy my hunger, but not one of my guests has yet laid a challenge down to another and until one does, no food shall pass my lips.'

'What form is this challenge do you speak of?' the Bishop asked.

Just as the King was about to answer, the great wooden doors of the hall flew open and there sat a pure white hare with emerald-green eyes. Silence fell, all eyes were fixed upon the hare as it hopped down the hall towards the King. When the hare reached him, it bowed a long and low bow and spoke in a soft clear voice,

'Great King! Forgive me for intruding, but word came to me, that here on this night, it is traditionally for one of your Knights to face a challenge.'

'Good Sir,' replied the King, 'No forgiveness is needed.! I am Arthur, King of these lands. My house is open to all. But pray, who told you of the traditions of my home? Come, sit with me and speak freely.'

'Good King! cried the hare, 'Your kindness and hospitality is known throughout the Kingdom and far beyond, it would be my honour to join you, but alas, I am on an errand for my master. I am here to ask if any of your Knights, who's brave and daring exploits far excel those from any other Kingdom, would accept the challenge of my master, the Green Knight?'

'No challenge will be refused my good Sir,' replied the King, 'as you have rightly pointed out, my Knights are the bravest in all the lands, to refuse any challenge would bring great shame to them. But pray, tell me of this Green Knight of whom you speak, for I do not know his name and of the nature of the challenge, so my Knights may know of what awaits them.'

'My master will soon be here, the east wind is calling his name now,' said the hare 'only he may speak of the challenge.'

In all the merriment no-one had noticed that the wind had started to blow, but now as they listened, they could hear the trees, naked and skeletal without their autumn cloaks of red and gold beginning to crack and groan as the air whipped round them and a strange murmuring sound, like the whisper of a name in the breeze.

The hare began to hop back up towards the door, as if to welcome his master, but as he reached the opening, a bright green light filled the room, stretching into every dark corner and the hare began to grow. The guests were transfixed, watching as the hare's back legs began to grow into the thick muscular legs of a man, its front legs into arms, its ears transformed in hair, until finally, stood in front of them, was an immense man with huge bristling muscles, legs like tree trunks and a chest that would have taken two fully grown men stood fingertip to fingertip to encircle it. I should say that he was more a giant than a man, such was his bulk! At his side stood his steed, a mighty horse, for only a mightiest of horses could have borne such a man. Never, had such a sight been seen in the court of King Arthur! The Knight was entirely green, his clothes, his skin, his hair all different shades of green, like the leaves of summer trees. He wore a tunic that fitting tightly around his muscular chest, a thick cloak hung around his neck, secured with a pin in the shape of a butterfly, encrusted with green gems. His stockings were as green as the grass in summer, but no shoes were upon his feet and no helmet on his head. He carried with him a single great axe, which too glimmered green in the light. His horse too was green, from hoof to nose, mane to tail. Its bridle and saddle adorned with the greenest of all the gems in the land. The whole court stood mesmerized by the man, who, followed by his loyal horse, now made his way down to where the King stood.

'I am Arthur, King of these lands and I bid you welcome,' said the King, 'Sit with me and partake of the feast on this night.'

'No, I am not the kind of man to sit about idly partaking of food and wine,' the Green Knight replied, 'You are an honourable King, across the lands you are revered, your castle is said to be the greatest in all Christendom! Your Knights are said to be the bravest and most true of all. I come to issue a challenge and to see if they are worthy of this fame. I have come here in peace at Christmastime, pray indulge me in this game, oh courteous and honourable King.'

'My challenge is simple; I will give my axe to any Knight and allow them to take but one hit at my bared neck. You have my word that I shall not flinch or pull away. The only thing that I ask, is that when a year and a day has passed, I should be afforded one hit at their bare neck in return.

The court was stunned into silence, no-one spoke, so the Knight continued,

'I never believed that one so great as the mighty King Arthur would be silenced by such a request, where is this bravery that is spoken of? You are no more a match for me than the housemaids in the kitchen.'

At this the King leapt forward and snatched the axe from the Green Knight's hand and raised it high above him. True to his word, the Green Knight bared his neck and prepared for the blow, remaining steadfast and unalarmed.

Just as the King was about to bring down the axe, Sir Gawain, the youngest of all the Knights, stood up and cried,

My King! I beg of you let me take your place, my life is worth nothing compared to that of you. Just as once my King, you pulled the sword from the stone and fulfilled your destiny, allow me the honour of slewing the head from this unearthly green beast and fulfil mine, however God should see fit.'

ORIGIN

by C. S. Parks

The soft snow made ascending the hill difficult and the winter's chill stung Bertilak's lungs as he quickened his pace. He noted the small dwelling at the top of the hill stood still, no sign of smoke coming from the chimney, unusual for this time of year.

He slowed as he approached the cottage, drawing a knife from his belt. He placed his other hand on the door and holding his breath he listened. A gentle sobbing pervaded from within. Bertilak pushed the door gently and stepped into the doorway, his frame filling the gap. He saw an old man sobbing into his hands, his lank, greying hair hanging loosely around his arms.

'Has she been taken?' Bertilak asked, although he already knew the answer.

The old man sobbed, 'I tried…he was too…he took my…'.
He lowered his hands from his face. The deep sockets were scarred and burnt; dark crimson tears stained his cheeks. Bertilak clenched his fists as his soul burned with rage and sorrow at the old man's appearance. He returned to his horse, spurring it towards to forest on the distant horizon.

The horse nickered as Bertilak approached the tree line that circled the glade. He felt his mount stiffen with unease and hesitation, slowing his pace as Bertilak dismounted. His destination was at the centre of the glade, where the old, ivy-covered chapel, known locally as The Green Chapel sat. Lowering in the sky behind him, the sun cast strange and disturbing shadows on the naked trees. They appeared to shiver with the approaching nightly frost. The landscape before him seemed to be a stranger to any joy that might be found in the world, bleak and colourless, except for the numerous holly bushes that seemed to fill the gaps in the trees, adding to the macabre scene; their bright red berries reminding him of the spray from the slaughtered lambs' necks during the culling season. A grim sense gnawed within his stomach, He steadied himself, as a man would stepping towards the gallows. A twig snapped underfoot as he moved across the threshold. The forest was alert.

Bertilak moved slowly through the trees, careful of his footsteps. He was aware that no birdsong or small animal scampered away on his approach. Occasionally, the branches of the trees would creak softly, as if being blown by the breeze, however, Bertilak noticed the air was still. He stopped to gain a sense of his surroundings. The top of the chapel could be seen a short distance away, the tree line seemed to close in around it, becoming exponentially thicker. There was a crack of wood from behind him; he turned drawing his knife. The tree line seemed unfamiliar as if the landscape had shifted. He felt lost and full of despair. He turned to reorientate himself on the position of the chapel, as he did, he felt a sharp pain streak across his head, he fell to his knees. Blood ran down his face and into his eyes. He wiped them and wildly swung his knife from left to right, frantically trying to see his assailant. Another blow struck him across his back, knocking all the air out of his lungs. He lay, prone, his face against the cold ground, it felt strangely comforting as the warm blood from the gash on his head seeped out into a pool around him. He felt something tighten around his neck and slowly lifted him off the ground. Then his wrists were bound, and his arms spread cruciform. Through one swollen eye, he could see the architect of his fate. Another branch slammed into his ribs, exploding what little air he had left in his lungs. He tried to breathe but his punctuated lung refused. Another blow to his abdomen and another to his head, and another somewhere he couldn't tell. Barely conscious he was aware he was being dragged along the forest floor, the indiscriminate holly bushes tearing at his flesh, determined to have their pound's worth. Finally, he felt his body move swiftly through the air and hit the soft grass outside the treeline. His only thought was he had to save her, he had to get to the chapel. He reached out in front of him, broken fingers dug into the dirt, and he pulled himself along half an inch towards the treeline. Again, they dug in and pulled another half inch. Once more he dragged his broken body closer to the treeline; and then his world went dark.

A curious sound roused Bertilak, a soft melody with an ethereal quality. He felt a warmth on his lips and a small amount of liquid entered his mouth, reviving him a little more. He carefully opened one eye. At first, he could only focus on the raven-haired head that was gently singing over him. She mopped his brow with a cloth. He noticed the dark purple of her eyes. Bertilak noticed that it was now dark and her pale, porcelain skin shimmered in the moonlight. She noticed that he was awake and smiled.

'Are you Fey?' Bertilak's voice was hoarse and dry. She nodded.

'You are the bravest soul I have ever seen, even at the edge of death you still tried to enter the forest. Can I ask why?'

Bertilak told her of the Sorcerer and of the lady that he needed to save. She told him of his injuries and how she had kept death a heartbeat away. She offered Bertilak a deal. To heal his wounds so he may fight for his love in exchange for his soul, to judge the bravery and honour of men for eternity. Bertilak wept and solemnly agreed. His world went dark once more.

An owl? Bertilak thought as he was awoken by a distant hoot. He sat up, expecting pain but felt none. The woman had kept her promise. On the ground next to him lay an axe. Its blade gleamed in the moonlight. He picked it up, swinging it a few times. It was crudely made and felt ancient, but the craftsmanship that had gone into balancing the weapon was sublime. Bertilak once again stepped across the threshold, Frosted leaves crunched under his footsteps. The forest stirred once more, a ripple in the tree branches readied Bertilak for the coming onslaught. A branch aimed at Bertilak's head, he raised his arm to protect himself and the branch struck it. He felt no pain. He looked at his forearm for damage. It had become covered in bark. Another branch struck, and another, and where each blow struck his body became covered in a layer of bark, however, his limbs still moved freely. Soon his entire body was covered in oaken armour. Finally, as one thick branch swung towards him, he countered with a blow from his axe, severing the branch from its trunk. He moved forward to another, larger tree and struck the trunk, the keen blade sliced the base open easily and an amber sap started to pour out. Bertilak moved forward again, only this time the forest seemed to shrink at his approach. Eventually, he stood at the edge of the glade. The chapel sat several metres away, an unearthly chanting coming from within.

Bertilak slowly pushed open the chapel door. It felt strange as he grew accustomed to the oak gauntlet that now seemed fused with his bones. He stepped into the doorway, ducking as he went through. He saw the lady in front of him, laid out on the chapel altar. Her flaxen hair hung over the side of the altar, She looked serene, dressed in a white gown. Candles flickered nearby, giving an impression of movement on her face. Half-hidden in the darkness, a stone throne could be seen on the other side. The chanting that was coming from shadows halted. A pale face slowly emerged into the light. Two dark, beady eyes loomed large in its sunken features.

'Impossible!' the sorcerer hissed as he leapt over the alter, his physical form twisted and changed mid-air. His new serpentine shape coiled around Bertilak's body and started to crush inwards, tighter and tighter…but the oaken armour held, rigid. Bertilak laughed, flexing his muscles, loosening the sorcerer's grip. He slunk back to the altar, cursing at Bertilak. A knife appeared from under his dark cloak, he held it towards Bertilak, then realised the futility of his actions. He turned and raised it above the lady, ready to plunge the steel into her breast. Bertilak acted quickly talking one step forward, swinging his axe in a wide arc. The axe eagerly bit through flesh and sinew, one cut removed the sorcerer's head from his shoulders.

'You have been judged and found wanting. There is cowardice in your soul', Bertilak said, as the body hit the floor. The head rolled some feet away.

Bertilak lifted the lady off the altar, carrying her through the forest in his arms. The trees seemed to bow and form an arch in reverence as he passed. At the tree line, the lady awoke. As Bertilak told her of his tale, she wept, her hand touching the bark where his face once smiled. With sorrow in their hearts, they parted. The forest embraced Bertilak as its new lord.

Bertilak returned to the Green Chapel and sat on the throne, he sighed and propped the axe next to him. He closed his eyes, and his world went dark.

Winter tumbled into spring, which in turn courteously bowed to summer. Autumn chided summer for its hedonistic ways and stoically prepared for the coming winter. Bertilak slumbered peacefully for the year. Bight green moss filled the cracks in the oaken armour and some shoots had taken hold on top of his head. He opened his eyes, taking a deep breath, filling his lungs.

The Green Knight rode out to the yuletide night, intent on challenging the bravest and noblest Knights in the land.

GRINGOLET THE GREY AND THE WILY WITCH

C. B Linford

A little different from a retelling, I found intrigue in Gringolet, the trusty steed of Gawain. Often times portrayed as utterly beloved in all renditions of Gawains' story, I knew I needed to give him a voice; for even those deemed unimportant sometimes have the most interesting of things to say.

On a clear winters morning when only the birds had begun to stir, the wind whispered mischief as it whistled through the turrets of good King Arthur's castle. His court lay sleeping unperturbed, while a witch crept their halls. She slipped inside Gawain's sleeping chambers, brushed a wrinkled, knobbly finger over his fair head, and then stole him away into the day; leaving not a trace behind.

At first the King thought he was sleeping, and then thought him ill. When Gawain came up missing and search efforts empty, the knights of the round table were roused to roam the kingdom and find the King's soft-spoken nephew. A day passed, and then three. Then seven days had passed with no sign of the knight. Not even a strand of hair.

Whilst all this was happening, one fellow fretted the most; a dapple-grey stallion who knickered and knocked at his stable door. His large ears flicked and lay flat at his helpless situation, mourning the loss of his rider who he loved so much.

On the night of the seventh day, Gringolet was stirred in his stable by a strange little light. It glimmered gently, *like a star in the sky*, he thought. When it settled upon his stable door, it became clear that the star was a fairy. Her white eyes glistened with worry as she fiddled with her pale petal-skirt, greeted the horse with a curtsey then spoke; her voice like the tinkling of tiny bells.

'Fair steed of Gawain, I bring to you a quest,' she spoke, soft and sweet.

Gringolet stamped his hooves, snorting with impatience. 'Speak.'

'Your rider does sleep,
In the restless dark deep,
Buried 'neath sky kissed stone.
A great lizard waits,
Broiling with hate,
Save him! Or he will die alone.'

With her poem delivered she curtseyed again, and her wings carried her into the air. She flicked her wrist, releasing the bolt of the stable door, then perched on his velvety nose. 'Good luck, Gringolet, and do not get lost on your way. Should you head north, a guide of your guise awaits you. Farewell!' She fluttered away, and Gringolet emerged quickly from his stable at a steady trot, setting out into the dark of the night.

He travelled five days alone, north and north again, until he was walking the muddy lochs of the Scottish moors. As promised, in the distance he saw a horse. Her coat was as black as the night sky they stood beneath, beckoning him from the path with a toss of her obsidian mane. He grew closer, hooves sinking and squelching in the thick, deep mud.

'*You are Gringolet*,' the mare stated, and began to walk. '*Come.*'

Mesmerised by her shimmering silky coat, Gringolet followed her. He didn't question how she seemed to leave no hoofprints in the mud, nor that they were no longer moving north; and nor why, with deep, watery black eyes, she was leading him into the loch. Her rippling muscles seemed to move with the water- and when he came to, it was too late.

He reared up high with a whinny of dismay. *'Sorceress- fae! You will not stray me from my path!'* he spun about on his hooves and made for the shore, but kelp grabbed his legs and dragged him down, his heavy feathered feet sinking in the sticky muck. The Kelpie let out a hiss, then moving as smoothly through the dark loch as a hot knife through butter, her lips split from the corners to the very border of her jaw, opening like a snake, revealing rows upon rows of sharp teeth.

'You are mine, Gringolet, there is no escape!'

Before he could feel the crunch of her maw upon his dappled hind, a silvery light came shining from the shores of the loch. The kelpie shrieked and retreated from its painful glow, dipping beneath the lake; and with great effort Gringolet shook loose the kelp, climbing slowly back to shore. His breath misted before him as he huffed for breath, staring in wonder at the being before him.

'I am Gwynth,' spoke the unicorn, her dazzling white coat like moonlight on a lake. *'And I am your guide. Silly Gringolet- has your knight not taught you better than to stray from the path?'*

If horses could blush, he would have. Instead, he hung his head. *'I owe you my life. What would you have in return?'*

She shook her head and turned, leading him back to the path. *'I would have nothing but our shared victory. Our quests align; the witch who stole your rider is the foul dragon who guards him! She has terrorised my people for centuries; her name is Bertel.'*

'A witch!' Gringolet exclaimed, tossing his head with exasperation. *'But what would a witch want with my good Sir Gawain?'*

'She wishes to consume the goodness in his heart, as she consumes it from my own kind. She will not stop with Gawain.'

Their journey took them through wolf-infested woods, their howls reminding Gringolet of his last adventure with Gawain, to the strange Green Man who had filled his rider with the scent of shame. When the sun rose again, they had reached their destination.

Gringolet shied back as he gazed up at the tremendous mountain, stretching into the sky, the dragons lair a yawning cavern mouth ahead of them.

Gwynth turned to face the dappled stallion and pawed a cloven hoof firmly into the ground. *'Are you ready, good Gringolet, to face Bertel in her cursed form, and rescue Gawain?'*

Without hesitation the stallion reared onto his hind legs, kicking his hooves out and shaking his great head. *'I am!'* He exclaimed, and then the thundering of their hooves echoed among the highlands as they galloped for the lair.

Without hesitation they breached the mouth, and immediately Gringolet leapt over the scaled tail of the dragon-witch. A deep scarlet red, it shimmered like rubies in the sunbeams that simmered through the cave opening. At the very back of the lair, suspended mid-air like a puppet on a string, was Gawain.

Gringolet loosed a squeal of rage and continued the charge.

Ahead of him a leathery wing lifted to reveal the open maw of the dragon-witch, Bertel, who rumbled deep in her chest, so deep that Gringolet felt it tremor through his body.

You Dare... Her gravelly voice seemed to resonate directly into his mind.

You Dare... Fickle Beast... To Challenge Me?

'I dare! Return to me my rider!' Gringolet roared and leapt upon the near mountainous hoard of twinkling coins and treasure to swing around his hind and hurl a well-aimed kick at her hard snout. His strike landed true, and she recoiled with a snarl.

Gwynth followed soon after him, prancing from atop the hoard of coins as though she believed she could fly. Her head bent down, and her long horn began to glimmer silver. Just as she was about to plunge her horn into Bertel's chest, the creature swung about her giant head and clamped her jaws shut around Gwynth's body. Silver blood splattered the ground as she hurled the fair being into the closest cavern wall.

'*No!*' Gringolet cried, and then took up the hilt of a sword half-buried in gold by his side. With a heave he yanked it free, then his hooves clobbered the ground as he made for the writhing Bertel.

Across the cavern, the silver glow had not yet diminished. Gwynth, nickering in pain, pushed herself to her forelimbs and instead aimed her horn at Gringolet. She fired a spell which consumed him in silvery light. Bertel dipped her head and lunged forward like a snake to make the kill, but suddenly swifter than ever before on his hooves he leapt aside and stayed on course for his target. Sliding to a halt before her weak underside and chest, he swung his head left, then plunged the sword firmly right- feeling the give of flesh crunch beneath the glowing blade.

Bertel let out a screech unlike anything Gringolet had heard before; a spray of billowing flames erupting from her jaws as she recoiled from the stallion. She grasped at her chest with twisted talons, clawing at the blade embedded firmly within- then fell, thudding down as a felled tree in a forest.

All was silent a moment- and then a second thud followed as Gawain was finally released from her spell.
Gringolet turned quickly to see if Gwynth was alive, and she was! Wounded but well, limping toward him with victory shining in her eyes. His friend okay, he allowed himself to rejoice, and pranced like a foal to his waking rider, who threw his arms around the stallion and laughed a laugh so loud and jolly that it made

Gringolet want to leap.

'You saved me, dear Gringolet- you saved me. As you toiled and strained to carry me on my quest to the Green Knight, now you come for me on your own quest. What a blessed knight am I to have such a loyal friend at my side. Such a tremendous, mighty steed!'

The stallion pulled his rider close with a tug of his chin, a tight embrace between rider and horse. He watched with warm eyes as Gwynth bowed her head and left, leaving nothing but cloven hoofprints behind her.

And soon, too, did Gringolet and Gawain return to Camelot, a great festival held for the hero-horse... who feasted on sugar and fruits for the rest of the year, praised and petted and loved by all who loved Gawain, and most especially by Gawain himself.

POETRY

Take time to let the rhythm of our poets' words wrap round you.

NO HOPE LEFT

by Amy Susana Cornock

There's that new boat with no name.
My school competition will soon announce
a Laura, Lizzie, Sandra or Suzie?
All on her own, she stands out from the crowd.
Her red and white hull brightens up
the witch wart green water.

A trolley pops out of the reeds like a metal crocodile.
The Monster Munch play piece swallows the swan's Sunblest.
Her engine roars, the reek of smoke soaks the sky,
the clogged tunnel fights to drain the gross water,
the end of her journey gets closer and closer.

No hope left. That new boat with no name.

There's that girl with the ripped tie
sitting on the same bench, staring at my stern.
As they approach she turns into a leaf.
The steel caps kick and
her stems hit the gravel and

her sap seeps out and
the water dyes.

Her body lies twisted like the roots of a tree.
Cries echo along the empty towpath,
a sheep dog barks for his master.
'What happened dear? Have you been attacked?'
Her eyes won't open. All she sees is black.

No hope left. That girl with the ripped tie.

CHOCOLATE ROOTS

by Amy Susana Cornock

The first time we met
you were a fountain of dark
liquid lashing down
a river without reason
within that sweet shop.

Fingers melting,
merging with the flow,
the ephemeral kiss of heaven
creasing my lips,
soaring me back to your roots.

Bitter bites of cacao, your forbidden
fruit as red as a ruby,
shedding seeds into the soaking soil.

Your wrapper gleams in the sweet shop
teasing those who dare to reveal
the dream of returning to the promised land
full of decadence.

A million miles from this shameless place
A million miles from this emptiness.

THE LUCK OF A DOMINO

by Amy Susana Cornock

The wooden box lies like a coffin
of mummies stacked in a pile,
starved of light till
she slides the lid and spots a symmetry of six.
Her fingers caress the cold ivory inlaid,
her tips trace the sunken spots.

She scatters them like seeds on the oak table,
her grandad's bony fingers start the shuffle.
The tiles clack like shells on the shore,
she takes a boneyard pick, deep breath.

Double blank. She's last again.

AS I WALKED

by C. B. Linford

As I walked along the path one night,
I came across an unusual sight;
Three men lay bare, stripped down to their toes-
Smothered in blood, brutally exposed.
I approached with a shudder, glancing over my shoulder,
And crouched by the closest who was pale (and a'goner,)
I whispered with haste- 'What a terrible fate!'
Then made onward my way to the village.
The murmurs soon spread of their gory demise,
Their bodies removed, and burned (as was wise,)
For England is wrought with terrors and fears,
And such evil things bring children to tears.

As I walked again one fateful dusk,
Along that pathway, walking brusque;
I came again across a corpse,
Separated from his horse,
Knew at once, we had a pest-
Then ran once more! Fled to my nest.
A party was formed, but not for fun;
To hunt the creature till it were done.
The men set out with pitchfork and torch,
Left their wives to worry on their porch.
And I, well I, of course I watched after;

For there goes the party alight with black laughter-
And shouting with will to put the beast down,
And rescue the men in this little town.
They searched for days, and weeks, then tired-
Returned from their hunt no longer inspired.
They hemmed and hawed and shrugged and slumped,

For no creature was found, they were utterly stumped.

As I walked the path due nightly,
I ensured my toes trod very lightly.
Behind me a trotting, a huff, a growl;
A barghest did follow, a shuck did prowl.
Gaze firm-forward and striding pursed-lipped,
I ignored its nuzzling and muzzling and nips;
The black dog it shook, and snarled and stomped-
Accompanying me on my evening tromp.
For the shaggy ghost-dog bears no ill-will-
Toward women who walk upon its pathed hill-
He herds us well home with a yip and a snap-
While real monsters stumble... right into his trap.

STOP RAPING THE SKATE

by Leola Rigg

Drop the dead weight trawl doors to haul iron chain and balls for plunder,
they sweep and crawl, ants seeking crumbs in kitchen's peace,
across an ocean shattered and neatly fleeced,
habitats harrowed asunder before we'll call humanity's blunder.

Stretch the footrope wide, feed it scope, drive hard and dig in deep,
scrape in all the fauna, shipwreck the flora, rev the donkeys of man's downfall
and treat the trapped to a braying sleigh ride to Pleasure Island's pride; haul,
crush the fish and drown the mammals that aren't for keeps.
Snap off ancient coral heads, smash them into smithereens,
obliterate uncharted underwater wonder,
nab them and net them, for the foreign fishmonger,
turn the seabed over, hear the piping plovers' tweet - no sea bream
and not a sole to be seen.

Wipe the slate clean, for the living are now the dead instead,
all mauled in the trawl; turtles, dolphins, whales an' all.
Remind me. What percentage is bycatch overall? Let the discards fall
astern, keep the blood from off your face, dress the fresh bedstead

with many a deadhead.

But don't forget, before you fling 'em back in, by the keg,
to cut the fins from off the sharks; what a bloody lark
to see their silly wriggle slide down to the dark,
washed and dressed in ocean tears, they sink like nets with lead.

The trawl footprint is an irreversible pall,
the hold is gorged, laden load line laying low, white wake washing,
a hissing snake,
a mirror image, contrails claim a widening wake,
decrying mass slaughter from every quarters call.

Can't we stop raping the skate for cod's sake,
is humanity fast asleep or busy being bleating sheep,
the sixth extinction is swiftly soaring, are our graves to be
mountain deep,
don't you hear the scientists say the whole world is at the stake?
Intergenerational effects are effectively mounting,
lost buoys baptise as water sprites and wanton kelpie's, to stiff
leftover fish a long time more,
synthetically synthesising destiny, wiped out by man's lack of
straight law,
to be sure, our methods for trawling are wacked and worse than
appalling.

Why can't we bear to broach and act upon the warning's truth,
will no stone lay unturned where man can't burn their deadly
flame,
when all is said and done in sums what hell is human's claim to
fame,
what's the bloody use in being us? The world's wildest animal on
the hoof.

An ever increasing, weeping sore on planet Earth,
our brains have gone to stuff, our brawn left at the door,

modern life our very own self-created flaw,
let's halt the horses before there's nothing left on earth;

but scurf and planet Dearth.

ASH IN THE AIR

by Leola Rigg

A zephyr in the air and all the ash blows,
smut grey soot swirling with an artistic flow.

Each particle a lithe dancer in the warming air,
choreographic from its fiery, febrile lair.

Until each dancer comes to gently rest,
black soot afoot upon the chimney breast.

A cloudy drift of wood ash in the grate,
and the ancient, stale smell from trees of late.

Ash fixes me in its grey stare,
spent dancers' slumber everywhere.

TRACKS OF DEATH

by Leola Rigg

Transcendental twanging, from electric wires up high,
Announce the tireless traveller, drumming on the track,
A snorting, wild eyed stallion, pounding hooves towards your
back.
Steel rails wail, steel wheels beat, a desolate die,
Blood bathed carriages, no soul to cry,
From blind white eyes, like tight binding crack,
This pseudo serpent comes headlong smack,
Surrounded by an ethereal sigh.

Quarter past every hour, a ruckus in our rural zone,
Luring lives on journeys ending, in a higher minding,
Riding snakebit through the meadow grasses, dead close to home,
Infernal manmade generosity, slyly winding.
Tracks like veins axe arteries, and turn my mog to only bone,
Every hour, I hear that steel grinding.

ALL ABOVE BOARD

by Leola Rigg

Government subsidies mean captains freely ease, mile long lines and trawls, as they please,
casting a strong, sticky web over Davy Jones head, to witless haul all the ocean, dodo dead.
Making way and wake to load their hold, cursing all who see these scenes unfold,
dredging deep for dregs of common skate, now rare, by our hand, Earth laid bare.
Government bills lack balls and brawn, by politics, not science, drawn,
'Limit the sale of that fish - (dispose of it as you wish).'
Codswallop and frozen prawns; they treat the sardines like pawns.
All hauled aboard, all trawled abroad, even the bycatch all above board.
Not fashioned for the fishes' farce, just the government havin' a larf.

SWAY UPON THE GREEN OF OLD

by Leola Rigg

With a skirt of white and a heart of gold,
they sway upon the green of old,
a skirt of a hundred petals all told,
hemmed in pink, good job I'm sold,
for the daisies grow twofold!

RAISE THE DEW

by Leola Rigg

A cockle-doodle-doo, wakes me and soon you,
to the first breaths of a new dawn promise, rising,
to banish the grey, ray by ray, and raise the dew
to a magical mist twisting and dancing,
among meadow grasses with a mystical view.

ABOUT THE AUTHOR

Peter Long

Pete has spent a long time figuring out what makes him tick. Writing has awakened something inside.

Compiling this book of stories has been a challenge, he had to be more organised than he's ever been before, but the stories needed to be told and this group need to be seen.

ABOUT THE AUTHOR

C. S. Parks

As an aspiring writer Chris has always show a keen interest in the many avenues this can offer. He has written poetry, short stories and songs. Some of which, it has been alleged, even make sense. He is inspired by writers such as Terry Pratchett and J R R Tolkien, and enjoys writing horror and fantasy .

ABOUT THE AUTHOR

Leola Rigg

Leola is most comfortable on the ocean wave, where she was raised and lived for much of her adult life, but she is now making amends with land, living in the countryside of Mallorca and learning to grow her own food and keep animals on her small farm. Her writing draws on all aspects of her life, an undying passion for the ocean and all the creatures within it and her  experiences on land, both good and not so. She is nearing completion of an Open degree with the Open university, studying a combination of environmental modules and creative writing, a hobby which allows her imagination to run with her pen.

ABOUT THE AUTHOR

Mandy Kerr

Mandy is a creative writing student with the Open University. She is a part time copywriter and full-time crazy cat lady who lives in Brighton and enjoys writing both humour and horror but hasn't yet managed to combine the two. She loves Stephen King and custard tarts but hates spiders and fruit scented toiletries. She is related to Rudyard Kipling and aspires to be one of Charlie's Angels (preferably Jaclyn Smith).

ABOUT THE AUTHOR

C. B. Linford

C B Linford is a young writer from County Durham in the North East of England. She's had a passion for story-telling and books since before she could even read (thanks mam!) and from the moment she could write, there was no stopping her. Her hobbies include gaming and archery, and she is also a keen artist, with a newfound interest in designing book covers. And now bookmarks.

Like all the other amazing writers in this anthology, she attended the Open University, studying her bachelors in Creative Writing, and at the time of publication is in her fifth year.

ABOUT THE AUTHOR

Laura Goodfellow

Laura completed a degree in English literature and creative writing with the Open University in 2022 and is continuing her studies with a Masters in creative writing.

Laura writes short stories inspired by her pagan beliefs, life events and her interest in stone circles and the history of witchcraft. She is currently working on her first novel inspired by the Pendle Witch Trials of 1612.

When not writing Laura can be found kayaking the seas and lakes near her home in North Wales or walking her dog in the Snowdonia mountains.

www. facebook.com/lauragoodfellowauthor

ABOUT THE AUTHOR

Christopher Beames

Christopher James Beames is an incredibly handsome man, gifted with almost unreal youth and beauty.

He hopes to find a way to translate this beauty onto the page and into the mind of those who desperately need it.

One day he will write the world's greatest novel; he just needs to find a way off his devilish, treacherous and cunning arch nemesis: the sofa.

Printed in Great Britain
by Amazon

38333287R10086